I0677861

They Gave Him Life!

Willie C. Harrison Jr.

DEDICATION

How can you reject the faith in God seeing that you were without life, and He gave you life? I asked God to accept this as having been done sincerely for His sake alone. I asked God to bring me its benefits during my lifetime and after my death. May those who read this book, print it, or have any role in distributing it benefit from it. May the peace and blessing be upon everyone that inspired me to go forth to write this: my story. May it help people to understand the life inside as well as outside of prison.

CONTENTS

ACKNOWLEDGEMENTS

I want to thank God first and foremost for giving me the time and patience to write this book.

Thanks to my wife who believed in me and pushed me. Cleaveria M. Harrison, I love you.

Thanks to my sister, Maria Studstill, for being in my life. I love you.

Thanks to my mom, Felecia Simmons, for giving me life and caring for me for all those months and not throwing me away, even after I did you so much wrong growing up. Thank you for being the strong woman God created you to be. I Love You! My brother, Urain Harrison If it's God will, you'll be home soon.

Willie C. Harrison, Sr., I love you, Dad! R.I.P

My little sister, Melissa Smith, I love you.

And to all the people who God put in my life, Thank you. I want to thank brother Dawud, a Muslim from Atlanta Masjid. Thank you for trying so hard to help me get back on my feet. I love you, Brother.

And to all that I didn't mention, I love you for the sake of God only! Thank you and may God's peace and blessings be upon you all!

CHAPTER 1
THE WORST DAY OF MY LIFE

It was Wednesday, November 8, 1989. Every morning in East Lake Meadows, as I thought about how I was going to get high, I would walk back and forth and wonder how in the hell I could get some crack cocaine. I would sit in a dark alley for hours waiting on my chance to trick someone so I could rob them, and then I would go over to Alston Drive which was another street in East Lake Meadows.

I heard these two guys asking for some breakdowns. Breakdowns are big pieces of dope that you can break in half to double your money. If you buy ten dime pieces of crack, which cost $10, and if they are big enough, then you can turn that into $20.

I stepped into action, "Hey, my nigga, I know where they at."

Some people were coming up to them, but

when you're on crack, you become a bona fide hustler. My crack knowledge kicked in. I convinced those guys that I knew where that fire dope was. They hesitated for a minute, but I was talking so fast and smooth that I convinced them to come with me.

I heard one of them say, "Man, he must know where that good dope at."

"Come on, man!" I told them.

We walked back towards Walton Lane, the side street where all my partners hung out. I'm steadily telling them that it's some good dope. "It's just right up here."

He asked, "How much farther do we have to go?"

"Man, I gotcha. It's right over here, around the corner." I said. One of the guys said, "Man, I'm not going around no corner!" I said, "Okay. Just wait right here. I gotta go get it."

Now, in my mind, I'm thinking, "Where can I go get a gun? I hope they got a lot of money. Ah, hell. I don't care if they have $20. I just need to go get me some dope, I'm about to rob these niggas."

I saw a stick and a towel lying on the ground. I thought about putting the towel over the stick pretending like it's a gun. But, if they had a gun on them, then they would have the upper hand on me. I needed a real gun.

When I walked around the corner, I saw my boy Tobie and he was cleaning his 9mm. "Hey, my nigga! Let me see that for a minute.

Tobie said, "I gotcha, here ya go."

"Lil Willie, it ain't but one bullet in there, man."

"F*** that. I'm about to rob these niggas. I ain't going to shoot nobody."

He gave me the gun and I ran back around the

corner.

"Give it up, nigga!" I yelled, pointing the gun at them.

"Man, you are crazy if you think I'm about to give you my money!" one of the guys said.

Pow! I shot that nigga. "You thought I was playing? Man give me everything in your pocket! Everything! Hurry up, nigga!"

"Man, you shot me!", the guy said.

"Nigga shut the f*** up! You want me to kill your ass? Aww, give me all the money!"

"Hey, man, that young nigga crazy! Give him the money." The other one said.

"Here, man!" The first one said.

The other guy started throwing money on the ground. "Don't shoot! Don't shoot!" He kept yelling.

I went through the first guy's pocket. He had a lot of money on him, so when I gave Tobie his gun back, I gave him some of the money.

There were a lot of people out there, but nobody really pays attention to something like that. You see it all the time. So, what the hell? Another nigga getting robbed. A lot of time, people were trying to get a piece of the action, hoping you dropped something, especially other junkies like myself.

People see things, but they kept quiet. If you were crazy and had a suspicious reputation, people were scared to tell the police anything if they come out there asking questions. "So, no one said nothing."

I ran through the alley to "the horseshoe," which was the nickname for another area in the Meadows where people would come and drive through to pick up a quick piece of dope. I ran through there hoping to see someone to take me to my grandmother's house in Kirkwood, off 2nd avenue. I saw Meatball, someone I knew.

"Hey, man. Take me to my grandma house, "I yelled.

"What you going to give me?", he asked

I said to him, "Man, I gotcha." Back then, people weren't saying, "I'll give you gas money." That wasn't important back in the 80's. People just wanted to make sure that you had money.

"Come on, Lil Willie." Lil Willie is what everyone called me because I was named after my dad. Yes, I'm a junior!

He took me to my Grandma's house. I went into the back room and took out all the money. It was $2000.00! "Oh, hell yeah! I'm rich!" I thought. I was so excited that I couldn't sleep.

I had something to smoke; crack rock, some weed, and some Newport's to put the crack in. When I didn't have weed, sometimes I would put the crack into the Newport's. That felt good putting the crack in the cigarettes. Then I would lick that cigarette, burn the sides, and burn the tip. I would lay back and, in my mind, it would seem as if nothing in the world mattered. I just wanted to get high for the rest of my life!

Thursday, November 9, 1989.

My Aunt Teresa told me, "Let's go shopping downtown!" She was so happy.

We went to the shoe store first. Back then, I loved some Stan Smith tennis shoes, Jordache jeans, and starter sweaters. I bought some clothes because it was cold for November, and I bought my aunt some shoes too.

We went and got something to eat at this Arab store and got some lamb meat. I guess this was my first encounter of Islam. Never in my life did I think that I would be eating lamb or goat meat. I asked for a lamb sandwich and then we got on the Marta train and got off at East Lake Train Station and we walked down to Cambridge Avenue, back to Grandma's house.

"Aunt Teresa, give Grandma this money. I'll be back later." I told her. I was about to walk back to East Lake Meadows.

"Okay," she said.

I walked down Second Avenue, thinking about the words of my Grandma." Junior, you need to get a job if you're going to be living here. "

"Okay, Grandma." Every time she would start talking about work, I would go back and live with my dad, and every time my dad would talk about working, I'll go back and live with my Grandma, hoping that she has forgotten that she told me a few weeks ago to go get a job

I wasn't thinking about a job. My job was to rob

and get high. A pocket full of money would make me happy as hell." I was going to get me some weed and some dime rocks.

This time, I had $500.00 left.

Three hours had passed, it was around noon on a Thursday. I was high and drunk. Time flew by fast. Before I knew it, it was 5:00 pm and I was smoked out and broke looking crazy. My eyes were bulging out of my head and I was back where I started from, trying to find a way to get another crack cocaine high or someone to rob.

I walked down on Evans Lane to see if I could see someone getting high in the "crack." We used to say "crack" instead of "alley."

I must say that I thought that the stingiest person in the world was a junkie. Even a person you've known for years would be totally against you once they got on that crack. They would dodge you, rob you, and they would even act like they never knew you.

I just started walking up and down the streets looking for a high, and I started getting madder and madder. I was walking through the crack from Evans Lane when I saw Buck. A week prior to that day, Buck and his boys pulled out a gun on me. When you're a junkie, everyone is totally against you. I walked around to where they were, and Buck said, "You need to get the hell out from around here."

"Man, you don't run nothing around here." I told him.

That's when he pulled a gun out.

"Okay, you got that." I told him, as I walked away mad as hell. I told myself "I'ma get that nigga!"

On this day, I walked around the corner, and

there he was, just standing there by himself. I walked up to him, stating, "What the fuck you want to do now, nigga?"

"Go head on, Lil Willie."

"Naw, man, you got a gun now?" So, I started to take off my shirt, and that's when he grabbed me, slammed me on the ground, and punched me in the mouth.

I jumped up and started running towards Evans Lane and I ran across Black and Mike. "Hey, man, give me a gun. I'm about to kill this nigga."

Black said, "Go ask my girl."

I ran up to Alston Drive and told Black's girl, "J, that he said for me to ask her for a gun.

She went upstairs and got a .38.

I grabbed it so fast and ran back down towards Evans Lane. I didn't see Buck, so I ran up to the side street, and that's when I saw Blackwell.

"Hey, I thought you let that shit go."

"Didn't I tell you I was going to kill you?" Pow! I shot once. As he turned, I shot him in the back, and he stumbled to the ground. I stood over him and tried to shoot again, but the gun wouldn't go off.

I started pouring the bullets on the ground, and, when I was about to reload the gun, a guy grabbed me and whispered in my ear, "Run, Lil Willie, run. Don't shoot him no more."

I ran one way, and Blackwell ran down toward Evans Lane. I ran about 30 yards and turned around. That's when I saw Blackwell on the ground. I started hearing everyone around him saying, "He dead. Lil Willie killed Blackwell. Lil Willie killed him!"

CHAPTER 2
IMMATURE

In 1986, I was 14 years old, going to Hooper Alexander Elementary. I was starting to be conceited. This girl was liking me. We used to talk all night on the telephone. We got on the subject about sex one night, and she told me she was going to give me some.

One day my mom went out, and I knew she was going to be gone awhile. I had to watch my sister, brother, nephew, and niece. That day, my girl told me to come over, and I knew that, if I didn't come over, she wouldn't give me none.

Laya is my baby sister. I asked her to watch my brother, niece and nephew. "I'll be right back, but, if Momma call, tell her I'm in the bathroom. Ok? I won't be long."

We lived on Memorial Drive at the time, and she lived in Royal Manor Apartments. This was a pretty good long walk, but I was a fast runner then. Beep! Beep! And I was gone like the roadrunner. Once I got there, we started kissing and hunching.

Then we stopped, and I called my sister Laya, to ask if our Momma was home.

"No! But she called and she wanted to talk to you. I told her you were in the bathroom, but she called right back. I can't keep telling her you in the bathroom."

"Ok, here I come." Instead, we went back to kissing.

This time, my sister called and told me, "Momma home." I was so scared. I heard her in the background yelling. She was furious, and I was too scared to go home.

I started praying. I didn't know what to do. If I go home, I'll have to find a new ass because my mom is about to tear this ass off. So, I called my dad. He was at work at the time. He was working for DeKalb County.

I called him, and I explained to him that I was over my girlfriend's house, because I wanted to see her. I didn't tell Momma because, every time I ask mom to go over my friend's house, she would say no. I had to juice it up a little to convince my dad to let me live with him. "Now she's mad, and I think, if I go home, she's going to kill me!"

"Naw she ain't." My dad said. "I'll be over there. You can come live with me."

I was scared but glad at the same time: scared to go see my mom, but glad that I'm going to live with my dad.

My dad came to pick me up, and we went to pick up my clothes. When we pulled up to my mom's house, all the lights were cut off. It seemed like a horror movie. I was scared to go up and knock on the door, so my dad walked up to the door. "Will you come on, Junior?" my dad said aggressively.

It was around 7:30pm, I knocked on the door, and my mom came to the door. "Where you been, Junior?" She asked me.

My dad said, "Go get your clothes, Junior!"

"Where you think you going, Junior?" My Mom asked.

The whole time I didn't say anything. My dad would intervene, and my mom was so angry. She started yelling, "Junior, you not going nowhere with him. I'm calling the police."

"Go ahead, Lisa," my dad said. "They can't stop me from letting him come live with me. He's my son, too."

My mom came upstairs and got in my face. "Where did you go, Junior, after I told you to stay home?"

"I don't know."

"You not going with him. You are staying right here." She went back downstairs.

My brother, sister, niece, nephew, and my stepbrother, Fonz, were in the house and in the room when my mom was arguing. She called the police.

My stuff was packed, and I started walking to the door. A knock came from the door.

My mom asked, "who is it?"

"DeKalb Police, Ma'am."

The first thing she said was, "I don't want my son going with him."

The police said, "Ma'am, is he the biological father?"

"Yes, he is, but I don't want him going with him."

My dad stood there smiling because he told my mom that the police can't stop him from taking me.

"Ma'am, by law, he has just as much right as you do. If he's the father, I can't stop him."

My mom walked real fast in the room and slammed the door.

The next day I was living in East Lake Meadows, the new kid on the block. I didn't know anything either about the street or about meeting new people. I was given a room downstairs near the kitchen. I came out of the room, and my dad came downstairs.

"You hungry?" He asked.

"Yes, sir."

"Well, go in the kitchen, and get something to eat then!"

Rene and Lil Robert came downstairs. Rene was my stepsister, and Lil Robert was her boyfriend. They had a little girl too. We all introduced ourselves. Then, I ate, sat in the living room, and watched TV. It was a Saturday.

Monday morning came around and my dad asked me was I going to school. I told him "yes." He said that he would take me to school. I had been living with my dad for about two weeks and I was still attending Avondale High School where I was in the 8th grade. When they found out that I was living in East Lake Meadows, I had to transfer to East Atlanta High School which was in that district.

CHAPTER 3
EAST LAKE MEADOWS
(AKA LITTLE VIETNAM)

"Lil Vietnam" is what we called East Lake
Meadows. This was a dangerous place because of a lot
of murders, robberies, rapes, and drug dealing. There
was a lot of other crime going on in these projects.
Anything you could think of has happened in East
Lake Meadows.

The biggest and ruthless gang, called "DBL"
(Down by Law), was started by a lot of gifted guys who
were good with their hands and feet. Some of these
guys were very smart, and some were even high school
graduates. You wouldn't believe, if you were to ever
meet any of these guys, just how smart they were. But
they just wanted to be part of something, and they
started a gang.

DBL eventually died off. People in other

projects around the City of Atlanta started forming gangs, and they went from fighting each other on the street to killing each other. Atlanta Police started to get involved, and a lot of guys went to prison for a long time. Some are even still there now. Some were killed. When that happened, twice as many disappeared. One was killed, the other went to prison."

All of this was before my time. I just heard so much about it that I was still kind of afraid, but I knew that once I got used to the people out there, then I'd be able to fit in.

My first day of school was like every first day. Everyone was nicely dressed, with fly shoes. It was as if everyone knew I was coming. I was being looked at strangely, the new kid in the school. Looking like a fool, I was green to the school code of dressing well. The reason for that was because we were poor. I didn't know how to dress that well. I guess that's why people were looking at me so crazy.

Well, not all of them. One day after school, I was on the school bus, and this girl, Shondra, said I was sitting in her seat.

"Find another, then!"

"No, I want my seat."

"Girl, go ahead on."

That's when she grabbed me, and I punched her. We started fighting right then and there. We were going at it, and everyone on the bus started watching it. She was getting the best of me. The bus driver stopped the bus and broke up the fight. That's when Shondra told me that it wasn't over.

When we got back to the Meadows, as soon as we got off the bus, Shondra slapped me and we went back at it again.

This time, however, another girl, Shay, broke it

up. "Y'all need to stop that." Little did I know that Shay liked me, and her cousin went with the girl I was fighting. We got close and started talking.

After we stopped fighting, once I got around the corner of Walton Lane, I started calling Shondra names, and she picked up a bottle and threw it so hard at me that it cut my head open real bad.

I was yelling and cursing at her, "I'ma get you. This ain't over." I ran into the house and started putting water and peroxide on my head. "Man, I'ma get her." I told myself.

Next day at school, I saw Shay, and we start talking. I asked her to come over to my house later when we get out of school. She agreed. We started dating.

A few weeks later, her cousin saw me. I didn't know at the time that the girl I got into the fight with, Shonda, was his girlfriend. I saw him on the porch talking with his brothers and Shay. Shay's grandma lived across the street from me, so I could see them talking. I saw Shay grab her cousin. I didn't know what they were talking about, so I went into the house and got on the phone.

I was still talking to Trish. We still used to talk on the phone all night, until one of us fell asleep.

The next day my cousin Reggie called me because he was in town and wanted to hang out. I was still new in East Lake Meadows. I didn't know anyone, so Reggie called me and asked to meet him on Memorial Drive. I was walking up towards Memorial Drive when I saw guys looking at me. I didn't pay it any attention and kept walking towards Memorial Drive. Then I saw some guys running around the corner. Once I got to Memorial Drive, Reggie got off the bus, and we start walking back down towards Walton Lane. Some guys got behind us, so I said,

"Run, Cuz Run!"

We ran towards my house. Once we got on the porch, one of the guys ran up on the porch and was about to hit me, and I saw my cousin about to hit him when Lil Robert came outside. He had about ten brothers, and all of them were big guys.

Lil Robert started going off on everybody, cursing them out, then he told me to come on.

We walked down the street, and he started talking loudly, and his brother must have heard him. What he was saying was, "If anything happens to him," referring to me, y'all are going to answer to Hodaddy." That was his nickname.

From that day forward, I didn't have any more problem with anybody. It was like everybody has been knowing me for years. I started walking around with the big head. Nobody could tell me anything.

I start hanging with this dude named Bobow.

We used to just hang around the Meadows and talk about people. We had nothing else to do, no life at all, until one day some big-time drug guy asked Bobow if he wants some work. When someone comes up to you and ask if you "want some work," that means they want you to sell dope for them, or with them.

Bobow started selling for this kingpin, and every time I saw him, he had a new car. So, I started wondering how he was able to do that. One day, I went up to his car. He acted like he didn't know who I was.

From then on, I started hanging with this guy Larry. We used to fight so much. We used to walk everywhere. I remember once, when we were at this store on Gresham Road, he started playing Space Invaders on an arcade game. He was hitting the button to blow the enemy up. I start mashing it, too,

"I got this, Lil Willie," he stated.

I wasn't hearing it. I kept mashing the button. Then the shooter blew up, and so did Larry. When I say, "so did Larry," I mean that he blew up in my face, that is, he hit me in the face. I punched him back, and we start fighting in the store.

Some guy said, "Y'all take that shit outside."

We went outside and started fighting. I hit him wrong and jammed my thumb, so I started running home. He began chasing me. My thumb hurt so bad.

A few days after that, I got into a fight with his cousin. It was like I was fighting every day. So, after months passed, I knew everyone in the Meadows.

One day, a guy called "Duck" brought me a cigarette and told me to smoke it.

"Man, you are crazy. Naw, man." I told him.

"It will give you a rush." He said, then he took the filter out of it.

I puffed hard and blew the smoke out. My head

was spinning so fast, but it felt good. From that day forward, I was hooked on Newport's. I had to have them.

I came home one day, and I left them on the table. My stepmom saw them and called my dad downstairs.

"Willie!" she said, "Junior is smoking Newport's."

"Well, as long as he buys them his self I don't care!" My dad said.

She was always hard on me, as if she didn't like me because I wasn't her child. However, her daughter, Rene, cared about me.

CHAPTER 4
LIFE IN THE STREET

The next day I walked up to Alston Drive, and I saw people walking up to cars. I was curious to understand why people would walk up to cars, so I met this guy named Kirk.

"What's up, man?" I said.

"Nothing. You want some dope?" He said.

"Man, you are crazy," and I said no.

"It's not like that. I mean, do you want to sell some dope?"

"How?" I inquired.

He explained to me how and what people were doing, and I started selling "dope" for him. Every ten bags I sold; I would get $10.00. I thought I was doing something because I was really hustling and making a little money now.

In 1987, I had dropped out of school in the

eighth grade and my dad didn't know. Every morning I would climb out my window and pretend to go to school and sneak back inside when my dad left for work. My dad must have known something because a few weeks later when I tried to sneak back in the window it was locked. When my dad came home from work that day, he asked me why I had left the window open and I played dumb and said, "What window?" My dad looked at me and said, "Don't worry about it." I would have to find another way to get back in the house, but I couldn't think of one. I just started hanging around the Meadows and waiting for my dad to come home. It was a while before my dad found out that I dropped out of school.

One day when I was walking through the crack of the Meadows, I saw this guy named Donkey and he was smoking something that smelled funny.

"You want some, Lil Willie?" He asked me.

"Man, hell Naw."

"It is nothing but weed."

At the time, I was smoking weed a lot and drinking beer: Bull, 8ball, Colt 45, and whatever I could get my hands on. Being introduced to this DOUBLE HIGH (crack and marijuana) changed my life. I eventually ended up on crack cocaine. I went from being called Lil Willie to Junkie Willie. It was as if I could not live without it, and I couldn't get off of it. The next day I started robbing people. I used to rob people who only had $10 and take it straight to the dope man.

I had to get me a rock and some weed. I found a dark spot in the crack in the Meadows so no one could find me and want some of my dope. All my friends were on crack cocaine, but I didn't find out about it until I got hooked on it.

The crazy thing about being on drugs is that it's

all about yourself. I was so stingy towards everyone because that's the mindset of Satan. He wants you for Himself. He doesn't want you helping people or having feelings towards anyone. It's all for Him to destroy your life. As long as I was on those drugs, I didn't care about anything else.

When you're a junkie, crack knowledge is serious. The only thing on a junkie's mind is getting high. I used to sell people peanuts in blue bags. They thought they were buying butter dope. They didn't know that I was selling fake dope. Once I gave them the dope, I would ease off slow because I didn't want them to know that I just flexed them.

I would go up to one of my partners' house and watch them get into their car and watch their face.

I would see them pulling out their pipe and put their rock on the pipe. "Shit! Man, this a damn peanut!" One of them would say to the other, "Man, how the hell you let them get you?!"

I would watch them get out of the car and go back to the spot where I sold them the flex, only to find me gone. They would walk for minutes and realize that they weren't getting their money back, so they would go to someone else. But next time they would taste the dope right then and there. They would shake their head and throw their hands up with the "ok," signaling to the other people in the car that it was good.

"What's up, Hershel?" I greeted Herschel, my best friend, who was also on drugs.

"Man, just trying to get that money up, so I can get me some dope." Herschel was a high school athlete. He reminded me of Hershel Walker. He was really good in football until he got caught up in the street with the wrong people. His life just went from sugar to shit. What I mean is he started out smoking weed and crack. He had always been a drinker of alcohol. Colt 45 was his favorite. He really was the one that got me heavy on the alcohol. We used to walk the street of the Meadows, looking for a high or some way to trick someone.

"I got an idea." Hershel said. "You got some money?"

"Yeah," I said.

"How much?"

"Just a few dollars."

We went up to the corner store. "Pop" is what we use to call this Chinese man. "Pop, what's up? You got some baking soda.?"

"Yeah, back there."

"Okay."

So back at my place, Hershel's crack knowledge kicked in hard. I don't know where he came up with this idea, but he put the baking soda we bought into a pot and boiled it, and it started getting hard. We took it off the stove, and he put it into the refrigerator. In about five minutes, it was hard like a rock. He put it on the table and started cutting it into blocks, and I started putting the blocks into blue bags. We went down on Evans Lane.

It was cold. We were out there for hours before we got our first customer. "How many you want?" We asked.

"What you got?"

"What are you looking for?"

"Dimes!"

"I got them dimes," Herschel said. "Well, you in luck tonight, I got you two dimes for $15.00."

"Man, is this some good dope? I don't want know bullshit."

"Man come on. You want it or not? Somebody else will get it. You think I'm out here freezing my ass off for nothing? Come on, man. Damn."

"Give me four of them."

Once they got in their car, we took off running.

Man, we hit a lick that night!

We went and got some weed and crack, then we found a good spot to sit and roll up the dope and weed together in the alley.

-I was sitting down crunching the rock cocaine up, and Hershel opened the weed bag and started pouring it into the leaf (weed paper). We were happy as hell, and about to get our smoke on. I was about to pour the cocaine on top of the weed in the leaf when a loud gunshot went off.

"Hey, niggas! Give me my money!

We ran so fast like we saw Jesus trying to save our soul, and we weren't ready to be saved. We were scared as hell. I ran one way and Hershel ran the other. I ran towards Alston Drive, and he ran down on

Evans Lane. Like I said, he was a running back in high school. He was running so fast; it was like he was running on water. I saw him, but then I didn't see him anymore. He was gone.

I ran up my friend Ron's house. "Ron, hey man, me and Hershel just tricked these niggas, and they after us!"

Ron said, "Just chill here."

"Cool!"

"You got some weed?"

"I got some dope, hell yeah."

We sat in his apartment and got high.

I was paranoid and hearing shit. "Did you hear that?" I asked.

"Man, you're tripping," Ron said. "Naw man."

"Hey man. It looks like the guys we tricked are in that car, and they are walking over here too!"

"Lil Willie, you are tripping, man. What's in

this shit?"

"I'm cool," Ron said."

I was high as hell, but I knew someone had jumped through the window. I know I wasn't tripping.

Hershel had jumped through the window. He said, "They were after me and I got away. I got the weed. Where's the dope?"

"Man, your hand's bleeding!"

"Man, I slid up under a car."

"So that's where your ass went. I saw you, and then I didn't see you no more. Man, you were running like hell."

"Man, fuck that! Where's the dope?"

"I dropped it."

When you get high, your crack lies kick in just to keep it all for yourself.

"Man, we need to get some more. I'll go get it." Hershel said.

"Man, you need to wait until the heat dies down."

"Naw, man, I need to get high."

"Ok, that's on you, man." I was really trying to convince him to stay, but we had been smoking dope all day. It is hard trying to talk someone out of not getting high when you're on that high roll yourself. There's no stopping it unless everyone that's selling dope has gone in for the night. "Go ahead, man. When you get it, I'll just come back up here later."

Hershel left and I went home... feeling... high.

CHAPTER 5
POINT OF NO RETURN

A few weeks had passed. It was late and I was looking crazy. I had no money and no dope, but I had some flex rocks in my pocket. It was like a ghost town that night. It was cold too. So, I started walking on Alston Drive.

This lady walked up to me. "Hey, you know where I can get two dimes?" She asked.

"Yea I got them!" I told her.

She looked at them and said, "Naw I'm good!"

I got mad then. I know I have to convince her to get these peanuts. Yes! Real peanuts: the 'Hershel trick'. "I gotta come up on her. I gotta have that money." I told myself. I mean, I really believed I was Satan that night. The only thing on my mind was the fact that she had $20.00, and that would bring some weed and rocks. "I'ma get that money," I thought.

She started walking towards Meadow Lake Drive. I started following here slowly, but she didn't know it at the time. When she started walking towards Memorial Drive, it started to get dark around that area because the streetlight was blown. She turned around and saw me. She started walking faster, and I did too. Then she ran into this yard which she must have thought someone lived there, but it was a vacant house.

I ran up on her and grabbed her. "Give me that money!"

"No! I ain't giving you shit."

I punched her and punched her, and for all I knew, I was just beating her, and she was screaming.

"Bitch shut up! You better shut up before I punch your ass in the face." At that time, I was only hitting her in the shoulders and legs and twisting her wrist trying to make her open her hand.

"Here nigga take, take it!"

I got that $20.00 and ran straight to the dope man happy as hell.

When I got to the dope man he said, "Damn, Lil Willie, you had to fight for this money. I see it got blood on it." I didn't notice that, but I didn't hit her in the face. At least that's what I thought. I just wanted that money, so I could get my high on.

A few months had passed, and there was this new kid on the block named Dusty. He was much older than me, and he was already on the dope. He moved to East Lake Meadows because his brother was going with this girl. He and I got extremely close. I considered him as being my older brother. We used to get his mom's van and just ride all over town listening to Public Enemy's *Don't Believe the Hype*. That used to be the jam.

We used to go to Bankhead Highway, and he

would rob people over there, too. I didn't care. We were like two peas in a bucket. When they saw us coming, they knew it was trouble. He started going with this girl, and he moved in with her. She was on the dope too. There were only a handful of people that weren't on drugs in the Meadows back in the 80's.

Dusty and I had driven around, getting high all day, I was all smoked out. I just couldn't get any higher, so he dropped me off on Evans Lane.

"Man, you sure you don't want to go over to my Mom's house and spend the night?" He asked.

"Naw, man, I'm good. I'ma go home. I'll be back over here in the morning. Okay."

The next morning around 8:00 a.m., there was a knock on my door.

"Okay. I'm coming, I'm coming I opened the door, and it was Stinky Man. "What's up?" I asked.

"Man, Dusty killed himself last night."

"Naw, man, quit playing."

"Man, I'm serious. He's dead.

I rushed and put my clothes on and went down to Evans Lane where his brother lived. I saw everyone on the porch, looking sad and crazy, and that's when I knew it was true. My big brother was gone for good.

I just cried all day and smoked out all night, pouring out beer and liquor and smoking rocks for my homie. "Damn!" I thought. I didn't know what I was going to do. My best friend in the whole world was gone. "Rest in peace, old friend."

One night I just stayed in the house, lying on the bed, looking up in the ceiling, thinking about the times we had riding, listening to Public Enemy, and thinking of places we'd go rob some people. That's when I heard shots outside my back door.

Two junkies got into it. This guy and lady were fighting because he smoked up all the dope, and she got so mad with him she shot him in the face. I was getting to the point now where I was tired of the Meadows. I was getting tired of doing the same thing every day to the point that I would go inside, get high, and start crying.

One day I started crying, and I didn't know why.

Duck, my other close friend, came up and asked, "What's up, Lil Willie? You alright?"

I just took off running, and he ran after me, but I didn't stop running and crying. I guess I was getting tired of the way I was living. I ran over to my grandmother's house and just sat on the porch. I just cried about being confused about life and having no guidance.

I would just pray to Jesus all night because that's all I knew to do at the time. One night my Aunt Teresa's friend, Tammy, had called to speak to her, but she had gone out to a club. I started trying to talk to her. She was going with this guy, Scooby. I wasn't thinking, or I just didn't care. Scooby had it going on, and he also lived in the Meadows. He stayed about a few doors down from me. I asked Tammy where Scooby kept all his money, and she really started talking to me like she liked me. I wasn't thinking either: she was a shake dancer, and they know how to trick guys, so she was leading me on. She said, "Okay, I'll talk to you later."

I walked back to the Meadows. The next day, I was standing on Evans Lane up under a tree where everyone hung out. It was still early, and I saw Randy and Polo talking, so I walked over and started talking to them. Scooby was looking at his car, and he signaled for Polo to come over, which Polo did. A few minutes later Scooby start walking over toward us. I wasn't thinking anything of it, but he walked straight toward me and swung on me.

I moved out the way and start running. Guys started coming out of nowhere, trying to catch me.

Ron came out and said, "Lil Willie, hey!" Ron was going to help me fight these dudes.

One guy called Peanut grabbed me. I started biting him, and he let me go. I ran for my life. I ran down Memorial Drive, and they ran after me.

Peanut grabbed me again, and Scooby was coming. I was fighting hard, so I managed to get away. I ran back over to my grandma's house, scared to death.

I went back to the Meadows a few days later, and I took a big stick. While walking towards Walton Lane, I saw Peanut, and I went at him with that stick and started beating him to death for trying to help Scooby jump on me. Later I found out that Tammy told Scooby that I wanted to rob him. I wished I knew where she lived. I would have jumped on her. I was in and out of the Meadows because I was dodging Scooby.

"Junior," my dad called me into the living room and asked me, "Did you go into grandma's purse and get her $5.00? She needed it for gas?"

I said "No, sir!" You know when you've done something wrong because that's when you get respectful. ("No, sir!" "Yes, sir!") But I knew I took it. I needed $5.00 more to get a rock. I got her money hoping I can go in with someone on a dime piece.

Once I got back to the projects, I ran into Hershel, and he had $5 dollars, so we went in on a rock (dime). After we smoked the rock, I went back to my dad's house.

He said, "Grandma said come over. She needs to talk to you."

Later that day when the sun went down

because I had to wait, because I was still running from Scooby, I went to talk to Grandma.

I was nervous, but I thought, "What the hell! I will hear what she has to say. She's probably throwing me out of the house or telling me I need to get a job."

I walked into the house, and Jackie and Teresa were sitting in the living room watching TV.

"Where's grandma?" I asked Teresa.

She said, "In the backroom."

"Grandma," I was calling her.

"Hey." she said

"Yes ma'am. My dad said that you wanted to talk to me."

"I signed you up for Job Corps. You will be going to Kentucky Morgan Field Job Corps. Get your clothes ready. You will be leaving in a few weeks"

"Yes ma'am." I was sad, but I couldn't refuse.

When that day came, she took me to the bus

station. Once on the bus, I saw that the whole bus was full of young people going to Job Corps.

THEY GAVE HIM LIFE

CHAPTER 6
JOBS CORPS (PRISON PREP)

I started talking to this girl. We sat together. But once we got there, we didn't see each other anymore.

I was placed into a dormitory, which was called "sticks." And they were the sticks! —rundown like shacks. After being there a few weeks, I got into school, boxing, and auto body. I let it all go except boxing. The other two weren't my interests. Fighting was my thing, I had a close friend named John, who was from Florida. We were bunkmates, and we did everything together, like brothers.

Being in this place (Job Corps) somewhat helped prepare me for prison. If you were from the South, you had to stick with those from the South. If you got caught by yourself, you were liable to get jumped on by those from the North and that's how it went down. The South against the North. It was crazy, but after learning how to box, I was ready to fight. I thought I was untouchable. It was like having a gun on you that you couldn't wait to use! I wished a nigga would try me.

After getting settled in at the stick's dormitory, we had a dorm rep. And he gave this speech. "Everyone listen up. Listen up! This is how this works. We have to live here together. We all have homeboys and girls here. There's a lot of violence going on here. Understand that the person that's lying beside you may be or may not be from where you're from. So, in here, we will learn to get along. I'm not having any bullshit in here. We came here for one thing, and that is to get our life together. Once we're done, we can go home and start our career or our own business. It's up to you. So, let's make the best while we're here. Now look around you. See who lives here with you. I

don't want no bullshit coming in here. I want you guys
to get familiar with each other now. I'm not having
this same speech again. Are we clear? Are we clear?"

"Yes sir!"

We were going to school or trade school every
day. After the day was over, we would just walk
around and see what we could get into: women,
fighting, getting high, etc.

One day, a few guys and I were walking, and we
saw a lot of guys hanging around this shed, so we went
over there and looked in. These guys were "running a
train" on this girl, and the next day, she was in the
hospital.

A few weeks later, a riot broke out. I saw John
fighting these dudes, so I joined him, and we threw
down. We went to jail.

Can you imagine that facility had a jail? Yes, a
jail. You go to jail and go to court, and it determines

how much you will get for the month. Every month you will get a check depending on your work ethic in school, your trade, and your conduct, etc. But every time you got locked up, they would deduct from your account. We already had the money in our account, but they would deduct from it if you went to jail.

After we were let out of their so-called "jail," we were sent back to the dormitory. A few weeks had passed, and another riot broke out. This time some guy that was in our dormitory and his boys who were from up north had jumped on John. John came in all bloody.

I asked, "Hey, my nigga, what happened?"

"Jersey and his boys jumped me.

"What?! Man, let's go get that nigga."

We were in the bathroom, and John was cleaning his face up. The dorm rep was also informed about the incident. About five minutes later, Jersey came walking in like nothing had happened, and he was walking down the hall towards the restroom where John was cleaning up his face. John started to walk out simultaneously as Jersey was walking out. Jersey was walking past the bathroom, and it went down. We beat his ass and everyone else's that was from the North. A riot broke out in the sticks. Officers came from all over.

"Hey! What the fuck is going on?!" The dorm rep shouted.

"Jersey and his boys jumped on John. He even got a kick."

We were back in jail, but this time, the judge told me that I had to go home, but I would be able to come back in a few weeks.

"Damn!" I thought. "I fucked up again! My grandma is going to be upset. She will think that I'm just a corrupt grandson. I just couldn't get it right."

Back on the bus heading home, I was now wondering what I'm going to do back in the streets. I had been off the drugs for months and gained my weight back. My grandma came and picked me up from the bus station. She just looked at me, and on the way home, she didn't say anything. There was silence all the way home. When we got home, I just put my things in the house.

Grandma then said, "You need to meet this man tomorrow. He will help you get back into Job Corps.

"Yes Ma'am."

The next day I went to meet this white guy, and today I still don't understand why I was going to see him. He was a homosexual. He had me cleaning his house, and he would pay me, but I felt uncomfortable going over there, so I stopped going.

I was back in the Meadows.

"What's up, Lil Willie?" Blackwell said.

"Nothing, man. Just glad to be home.

"Where you been?"

"Job Corps."

He laughed. "Job Corps. Ha!"

"Yeah! How's the military life been?"

"Man, I went AWOL."

"What?! Man, you crazy! You want to go get something to drink?"

"Yeah, why not?"

We went and got a Colt .45, and we came back to the Meadows and ran into other friends. I saw Hershel. He said, "Lil Willie, what's up, man? Let me holler at you." We went off for a while, and it was back to getting high, "back on the crack rock."

The next day I ran back into Blackwell.

"Lil Willie, where did you go? He asked

"Oh, just went to go holla at this girl."

"Oh, who's beeper is that?

"Oh, I found it."

"You want to keep this watch for it?"

"Yeah."

"Ok, man, don't sell my watch."

"Man come on we're friends. You think I'll do that to you?"

A few weeks had passed, and I ran out of money. I had the watch, so I sold it to a dope dealer. The watch was worth about $150.00, but I got $20.00 worth of dope for it. I just wanted to get high. "Fuck that watch," I thought. He had my beeper. He can have it now.

I got hooked up with this older chick, Pam. She was ten years older than I was, and we hit it off well. She was the older sister of a guy I knew called "Sticky."

She had an apartment in the Meadows. I was

on drugs. I didn't know anything about relationships, but I think I was in love with her. She had three kids by one guy.

I was in and out of the house at night. I was so confused, and we would fuss and fight all the time, but the whole time we were together, all she wanted was me to get my life together. I was just too messed up on drugs, I couldn't think outside the box.

I was on Evans Lane with some dudes trying to get some money when Blackwell drove by.

"What's up? Old fuck ass nigga?" I shouted at him.

He walked back around and walked right up to me and hit me in the face.

"What the fuck wrong with you?" I asked.

I swung back, and he hit me before I was able to connect to his face. I was dazed now, and guys start saying, "Man, y'all break that shit up?"

"Man, what the fuck you hit me for?" I asked. "Man, you play too much, nigga."

"Man, I'ma get your ass nigga," I said, and he hit me again.

I fell, and everyone started crowding around looking. Sticky came down there.

"Man, I'ma get your ass." I told him. I walked back up to his face.

"Go head on, man"

"Naw, nigga. You should've never put your hand on me."

He swung again and nearly knocked me out. I got up.

"Come on, Lil Willie." Sticky said.

I took off and ran towards Pam's house. I was looking for a gun, but I couldn't find one, so I got a baseball bat and ran around to where Blackwell lived.

He was coming out the house. "What's up now

nigga?" I said. "Man go head on." He said.

"Man, you should've never put your hand on me. That shit was fucked up," I said I think it was peer pressure more so than the actual fight that had me so angry and embarrassed.

"Look man. Let that shit go. Let's go get something to drink."

"Naw nigga you go ahead!"

We shook hands, and I went back to Pam's house. She doctored up my wounds, but later on we got into another argument.

She had given me some money to go buy some dope to "come up on," *i.e.,* to re-sell. Instead of doing that, once again I smoked it. She was upset, but I made it seem like it was her fault. I started crying and ran out of the house down towards Evans Lane.

A lot of people were down there, and I saw Blackwell. I was drunk and high on crack.

"What the fuck you wanna do now, nigga? I'ma get your ass, nigga! I told him.

"Man, let that shit go, Lil Willie."

"Naw man, you put your hand on me for nothing."

"Man, you better get the hell on."

People started gathering around. "Man, y'all let that shit go," Some of them said.

Mike and Duck came between us. "Come on Lil Willie," Mike said. "Let's go to Sharon's Showcase."

We drove there. I start walking through the crowd, and this guy bumped into me. He had on a gold gun necklace. I snatched it off his neck.

"What the fuck you want to do nigga?" I challenged him. Being that the Meadows was around the corner, we ran the Showcase. If one gets into a fight, the Meadows go off. We will turn that shit out. I started walking through the crowd until someone grabbed me around the neck. I thought it was that dude I snatched the necklace from. I turned around so fast, and it was Blackwell.

"Man, what's up?" he said.

I went off. "Man, what the fuck, nigga? I don't fuck with you, nigga."

"Man, let it go, Lil Willie." Duck said.

"Man, I don't fuck with you." I told Blackwell.

Duck, Mike, and I left.

CHAPTER 7
A BAD SITUATION

The next day I went shopping for drugs. When I came back into the Meadows, I saw Blackwell.

"Didn't I tell you I was going to kill you, nigga?!" He saw the gun pointing at him, and he attempted to run. That's when I shot once, and he fell. I ran back over to him shouting "Die, nigga, die, die!"

I called my uncle to come pick me up from my cousin house where I ran from shooting Blackwell.

"Man, for what?"

"I just killed someone!"

"What?!"

"Yeah!

He was over there in five minutes.

"Here, this is the gun."

"Man, what happened?"

"I don't know Unc, take me over to Trish's

house."

Trish was another girl I was messing around with. When I got over there, she was at work, but her mom and sister were there, along with her little girl, Tashona. I hugged and kissed her.

Then I called Pam. She sounded like something had happened to her.

"What happened?"

"Just come Home, I took my girls over to their dad's house because these guys been down here looking for you. They think you're in here. And the police been down here."

"What?!"

"I'll be over there in a few minutes." I hung up the phone and called my uncle Wayne back and told him to bring me a gun and a change of clothes.

He and his buddy came and brought me a .357magnum.

I went in the back way of the Meadows. I just started shooting at people I saw and screaming, "Where y'all niggas at now?" I walked up on Rodney, Duck and Toby. I pointed the gun at them and told them, "Don't run." When I got closer to them, I asked, "Where those niggas at?"

"Man, they around the corner."

I walked down on Evans lane, and I ran up on the hill where I saw a few people standing. I heard the police coming, but I was still high on drugs and alcohol. I just didn't give a damn. I was about to kill these niggas that were harassing my girlfriend.

Lil Robert came around the corner. He's Hodaddy's stepsister's boyfriend. "Man, get the hell away from here!" he stated!"

I looked up to him like my big brother, so I took off running back to my girlfriend's house. Duck, Rodney, and Tobie were still there, as I told them to stay there until I got back. I took a sip of bull, that's the beer I use to drink back then.

I started walking towards the back door, and that's when I heard a hard knock.

"This is the police! Open up!"

I ran in the back room. "Pam, don't open the door!" I told her.

"Open up!" The police stated. "We're about to knock the door down. Open up now! We know Lil Willie is in there. Open up now!"

"Pam don't open the door!"

I was in the closet hoping that she wouldn't open the door, but she was so scared, she let them in.

"Where is he?"

I was in the closet with the lights cut off. Two Atlanta Police Officers, one black, and one white came in the room with their flashlights and guns drawn

"Come out! Come out!" the black policeman

said.

"Don't shoot! Don't shoot!" I responded.

Once I came out of the closet, the black police officer started beating me in the head with his gun. My head just started bleeding bad. They had me handcuffed, and he just kept beating me until we got to the car. I was told that my uncle was about to jump on the police after he saw what the officer was doing and how he was beating me. He hit me in the top of my head so hard that I fell out and went to my knees. He pulled my arm, and I woke up. They threw me in their car and drove off.

The black officer was in a rage screaming at me. "Why did you kill him? Why you kill him?" He kept asking me. We drove behind Drew Elementary School, and he put the gun in my mouth and told me, "I should kill you. I can get away with it. I should just kill you, man. Why did you kill him?"

"Man, I didn't kill no one. I don't know what you're talking about."

"Shut up. I should kill you." He stopped the car again.

"Man, please don't kill me!"

We drove to the homicide office. They took me to the holding room. People started asking, "What happened to him?" Blood was all over my body.

A few minutes later, another officer came in there. "What's your name?" He asked.

"Aldo Harrison."

I forgot my uncle gave me his military jacket and his freaking license was in it, so the officer came in there and said, "If you're Aldo, who is this then?" He showed me my uncle's picture.

Damn!

Pam walked in. I was just sitting in that cold room with dried up blood on my face. She got some paper towels and started wiping off my face.

"What have you got yourself into Willie?"

I was just sitting there, not saying anything to her.

"Let's go." An officer walked in and told me.

Pam asked him, "Where is he going?"

"To the hospital."

They took me to Grady Memorial Hospital. Once I was there, they handcuffed me to a bed, and I was just lying there. I had lost so much blood that I started feeling like I couldn't breathe. I started asking for water, and a nurse brought me some water. A few minutes later, my Aunt Teresa and Angie came in there while the doctor was putting stitches in my head. He put 18 stitches in my head and wrapped my head up.

The police walked in, saw both my aunts in there, and aggressively asked them to leave.

"I'll see y'all later. I'll be up out of here. They don't have nothing on me." I told my aunts.

After the doctor was done, the police took me to Fulton County Jail on Rice Street. I stayed there in a one-man holding cell.

The next day, a lawyer came to see me with other people who had cameras. He started asking me questions. I didn't know who they were, so I started lying about what had happened between me and Blackwell. The lawyer and his crew left.

A few days later, I was transferred to DeKalb County Jail. I didn't know why. They booked me in. and about three days later, the officer said that I had a visitor

In my mind, I was thinking, "Who could this be? It wasn't the weekend for visitation."

I went into this room, and a lawyer came in. "How are you? Willie Harrison, right?

"I'm fine."

"Your grandmother asked me to come see you."

This sent up a red flag in my mind. I had asked my Grandma if she could afford to hire me a lawyer, and she said she couldn't. So, I didn't think that this was my lawyer because nobody in my family had that kind of money so when he started asking me questions, I didn't trust him.

"Willie, tell me what happened." The lawyer asked me.

But in my head, I was listening to those so-called "jailhouse lawyers." "Man, if you don't know who come and see you, don't tell them nothing about your case. They will trap you up, and in the courtroom, they will find you guilty. So, if you don't know who you're talking to, don't sell yourself out." This was going through my mind, so when the lawyer was asking me all those questions, I just lied to him.

He stood up and said, "Once you're ready to tell me the truth, tell your grandma to give me a call." He walked out and never came back.

I went back to my jail cell and called my grandma.

The first thing she said was, "Junior, why are you lying to the lawyer? He's trying to help you."

I called his office over and over, but no one accepted my calls. I felt screwed, listening to those no-good "jailhouse lawyers."

I called my Momma and explained everything to her.

I remember lying there in my bed, smoking a cigarette, thinking back on my life, and crying, "I'm never getting out of here."

Then, an officer called me. "Mr. Harrison."

"Yeah."

"Come up front. Someone's here to see you."

It was a public defender. The first thing she asked was my name. Then she told me to tell her what happened

 I just started telling her the whole thing, well, half-truth, at least. It was a lot different from the lie I told the first lawyer.

"Okay, Mr. Harrison. I'll talk with the DA and see what we can do to get you out of this."

I went back to my cell and called my Momma.

She asked, "Did a lawyer come and see you?"

"Yes, ma'am. I just told her what happened, and she said she'll see what she can do." I just started crying and apologizing to my Momma.

She said, "It's okay, Junior. I know. I know."

"Lock down," the officer start yelling.

"I love you, Momma."

"Okay, I love you, too, Junior."

CHAPTER 8
LIFE WITHOUT PAROLE

At my court hearing, I was standing in front of the judge and the DA while my attorney was explaining my case to them.

"Okay, Mr. Harrison, do you understand what's going on?" The judge asked me.

"Yes, ma'am." But I really didn't know what was going on. I was just saying yes to everything.

The officer took me back to my cell. My cell mates asked me, "Lil Willie, what are they talking about man?"

I rolled a cigarette and told them that they were talking about giving me two life sentences and 20 years.

"What the fuck, man? You better go to trial. It's hard to prove a murder trial. Don't let them trick you.

I'm not." Now I was really scared.

One day when I came out of my cell for rotation, I needed to make a phone call but there were two other guys already on the phones. We only had an hour to be out of our cell, so I asked them how long they were going to be on the phone. They both looked at me but neither of them said anything. I asked them again and they both ignored me again. I grabbed both phones and hung them up and we all started fighting

The guys in the dorm started yelling for the police because those two guys were tearing my ass up! I was glad they called for the police because those guys weren't playing.

The officers moved me to another cell, and I was in there with one of my homeboys from the Meadow. We were side by side, working out, laughing, and just tripping.

"Mr. Harrison, you have a visitor." An officer called me out of the dorm.

"Okay."

They took me to an attorney visit.

"Hi, Mr. Harrison." It was my court-appointed attorney. "I talked with the judge and DA. They said if you plead guilty, they will run the 20 years into the life sentence, and if you do three years on good behavior, you'll go home."

"Hell, no! I'm not pleading guilty. I killed him in self-defense. He jumped on me."

"Well, there were witnesses that said you shot him in the back as he was trying to get away from you."

"That's not fucking true."

"Calm down, Mr. Harrison. I'll go back and tell them that okay."

The attorney left, and I went back to my cell, waiting on rotation so I could call my Momma to let her know what they were talking about.

I came out on rotation. Once again, a guy was on the phone. They only had one phone working, so I asked him, "How long you going to be?" He just straight up ignored me, so I just slapped him. We were going at it, but this time, I was on top. The guys start yelling for the police. They came running, and by the time they opened the door to the dorm, we both fell out the door, and they broke it up. I was moved to another cell.

I called my Mom. "Momma, the public defender talking about, if I plead guilty, they will run 20 years into the life sentence, and I'll be out in three years on good behavior."

"Junior, just do what you have to do, and come home."

"Yes, ma'am."

On May 14, 1990, I was back in the courtroom. My girlfriend, her brother, my grandma, and the victim's family were also in the courtroom.

"All rise."

The judge walked in. "You all can be seated. The judge called my name, "Mr. Harrison."

"Yes, ma'am." I stood up with my attorney.

"I hear that you're ready to make a plea."

"Yes, ma'am."

"Do you understand that you're giving up your rights?"

"Yes ma'am.

We went on through the typical guilty plea questionnaire.

"Okay, I accept your guilty plea, and sentence you to life in prison. Hope all goes well. Take care."

"Yes, ma'am." I turned around, and my family and friends were leaving the courtroom with their heads down.

The victim's family was glad. I heard someone say, "That's what that bastard gets. I hope he never gets out."

I sat there looking up at the sky wondering what's about to happen with my life. I'm never going home. I had forgotten that the DA and public defender said I'll be out in three years on good behavior. When I remembered that, I kind of cheered up in my cell I rolled me up a good fat cigarette.

Someone asked me, "Hey, Lil Willie. What they give you?"

"Life!"

"What? Man, don't tell me you pled guilty?"

"Yeah. So, fucking what? I did it, so I'll have to do the time. Besides, they said I'll be out in three years or so on good behavior."

"What? Who the hell told you that shit?"

"The public defender."

"Lil Willie, you have a life sentence. That means for the rest of your freaking life. Damn, man! You messed up."

"Man, I don't want to talk about it no more."

I came out on rotation, and the guy who I was talking to was still in his cell.

"Lil Willie, throw this paper away." He tried to give me a piece of paper to throw away for him.

"Man, I ain't throwing nothing away. You'll be out."

"Man, don't take that shit out on me because you plead guilty to life, nigga."

"What, nigga?!"

"Fuck you, man. You're just upset."

I walked over to his cell and slapped him threw

the bars.

"Oh, hell no, nigga! I'ma fuck you up for that shit." He started yelling, "Officer!"

"Hold on, nigga! I'll go get him! Officer!" I started yelling for the officer to come let him out so we could fight.

The officer came to the door. "What's the problem?"

"Someone needs to talk to you."

"What cell?"

"Six."

He opened the door, and we went at it. The officer let us fight for about a minute.

We were fighting hard. I didn't even care anymore because, in my mind, I was thinking, "What if he's telling the truth about me never getting out?"

Other officers came and broke it up. "Lil Willie." One of them called me. "Man, you always fight. Go pack your stuff. You going to another cell."

This time, I was next to my homeboy, Randy. He was in for blowing a guy's head off. We were really cool. He used to look out for me in the Meadows when he would see someone about to mess with me. Now, he was crazy as hell. He even pulled out a gun on me because he thought I pickpocketed him for his dope. He was on rocks, too.

We used to trip all night until one day when he asked if he could see my radio. I told him, "I got you." I was listening to it.

He got upset, so the next day I let him see it, but he wouldn't give it back. We started arguing, "Man, I'ma fuck you up when I come out." I told him. We started arguing back and forth, but we never came out on rotation together, so we never fought.

One night, I was lying down when the front door to the cell opened. My name was called, "Lil

Willie."

"Yeah!"

"Pack it up. You're going down the road." In other words, I was going to prison.

I thought they would never say that. Instead, I thought they would say, "You made parole." Anyhow, I thought, "In three years, I'll be out of here. I'm going to keep to myself and get the hell out of prison." I grabbed my bible and the little things I had. I couldn't use the phone because they said that I was an escape risk, so I had to call my family after I got to prison. "Okay, I'm ready. Where am I going?" I asked.

They didn't tell you, but one of the worst prisons in Georgia at the time was Lee Arrendale State Prison, commonly called "Alto." It had a bad reputation as a rough prison with a lot of young and wild prisoners. Those young boys didn't play down there. So, when they finally told me that I was going to

Alto, I was scared as hell. My heart was beating fast, and I was afraid of never getting out because I would have to kill someone else if they tried me. There were about 15 teenagers on the bus, and we were all headed to Alto

CHAPTER 9
ALTO STATE PRISON: LIVE OR DIE

Alto was about a two-hour drive from DeKalb
County Jail, and I had to use the restroom on the bus
because I was so scared that I didn't want to use it at
Alto. When we pulled up, I saw nothing but barbed
wire everywhere. People were walking around on the
yard, and as soon as the bus pulled up, people started
coming to the fence that separated the yard from the
bus intake area.

"Hey, nigga! You mine." Some of them yelled to
some of us.

"Yeah, right." I said.

We all went into the ID room, which is what
they called the intake area. A big white officer came
out with a blackjack on his side and said, "Everyone
get naked."

I slowly started taking off my clothes, still

scared. Then we all got into the shower together. This was crazy. Once we got out, they made us put on this cream for lice or anything else that we might have brought in. "Everyone get in a line, and put your hands behind your back," they told us. We were going to the hospital floor. We all went up there and got a physical exam and an HIV test. The doctor was a gay, white guy they called Goldfinger. I hated him. I went in the room and he said, "Pull your pants down and bend over."

I said, "Man, you are crazy. You ain't putting no finger in my ass."

"Officer, I have a refusal!" He announced.

The officer came in, and right then, the officer and I went to blows.

"You ain't sticking your finger in my ass." I was yelling. Eventually, they got the best of me, so I went to the dormitory feeling raped by this gay doctor who we called Goldfinger. I think he gets a thrill out of sticking his finger in guys' butts. I felt terrible.

We walked backed to Dorm 6. It was the diagnostic dorm.

"Willie Harrison." The officer called me to the front after I put my bags down.

I was escorted to the counselor's office. I walked in. Counselor G is what they called him or what he called himself. "Have a seat." He talked like he didn't play any games.

"Yes, sir!"

"Now I have your file here."

I was wondering when I created a file so big. I had just gotten there.

He started looking into it. "I see you have been doing okay, so I'll recommend that you go to the good dorm. You have to keep a good record so when you come up for parole, you'll make it, but so far, you're looking good. Okay, I'll see you around. If you need anything, let me know." That was a lie though.

"Yes, sir!"

I was escorted back to the dorm, and I sat on my bed and started reading my Bible. As time passed and new guys started coming in, I started preaching the Bible to them and I started having a crowd around my bed. I had the Holy Spirit. I really felt that by my preaching to the guys that Jesus was going to let me out of that place in three years.

"Inmate Harrison, EF 259694."

"Yes, sir."

"Pack it up. You moving to population."

"Where I'm going?"

"Man, you don't know. You'll see when you get there."

Now, at the time I went to prison, there were only white guards, and they were racist people. They loved their job. I went to the worse dorm in population, Dorm 14, the "dog pound," they called it. Counselor G said that I would go to a good dorm, but being that I had life plus 20 years, I wasn't qualified to be in a good dorm until I been there for a while.

I went to the dorm, put my bags down at the door, and everybody started looking at me.

"Hey, y'all. "I heard someone say. "New ass coming in."

I was nervous, but I couldn't show it. The dorms were open dorms, like army barracks, not two-man cells. About 150 people were crammed into such a small place like sardines.

"Inmate Harrison."

"Yes, sir."

"What's your EF number?"

"259694."

"Ok, you're on bed 33, top bunk. Odd beds

were the top, even beds on the bottom.

I started putting my stuff in my locker, and guys started coming up to me asking me where I was from.

I said, "From Atlanta. The Meadows."

Someone said, "Hey, Ray, you got a homeboy over here."

"Who?" Ray asked.

"Your man, Lil Willie." They told him.

Some guy called Ray came over and started questioning me like he was the police, so I played the role. I started meeting a few people after I put all my stuff in my locker box. I sat on the bed and started reading my bible, waiting on them to call chow, which means mealtime or time to eat.

This was the worst food in the world. Our stomachs really had to get used to this type of food. When I first ate this food, I was so sick I went back to the dorm and threw up. It seemed like I spent an hour over the toilet. Someone came into the bathroom.

"What's up, man? You alright?" He asked.

"Naw, man. This food is terrible."

"How much time you got?"

"Life."

"Well, you better get used to it cause you ain't never getting out."

"Yeah. I guess you right. Damn! This shit is nasty."

"Unless you make a store call, you'll be eating a lot of the food in the chow call."

"Yard call. Who's going out ladies?" The officers would call a lot of people in the dorm "ladies." To them, it was like a joke. I never liked for the officer to call me that, but I was new. What could I say or do? Plus, the officers at Alto had it where they would bring guys stuff from the outside world, like food, weapons, *etc.* If you got into it with the wrong officer that had a reputation in the prison system, you might find yourself dead or stabbed, unless you just had that reputation, too. I just went along with it. I was trying to make parole in three years.

CHAPTER 10
I GAVE UP

Vocational school, or what we inmates called trade school, was called at 7:30 in the morning. This is where you could take brick masonry, auto body, barbering, etc.

I was having this problem with this guy named "Kel." He just felt like he could just talk to me any kind of way, but I was trying to stay out of trouble because I didn't want to mess up my parole. I tried to ignore him a few times, but it was really getting to the point that I wanted to hurt him. One day in the chow hall, he came up to my table and stuck his finger in his nose and put it in my grits. Everyone just started laughing. I was so freaking mad, but the only thing on my mind was just trying to make parole.

My homeboy Donkey was shipped to Alto. He was from East Lake Meadows. He got there and started bullying people. He was about 6' 9", kind of big. He didn't play. I saw him and told him that I was having problems with this dude, Kel.

"I'm about go bust this nigga in his head tonight." I told Donkey.

"I don t blame you, Homie. If the nigga trying you, do what you have to do."

"I'll talk with you later."

"Heading back to trade school, I stopped at the window and started talking to another one of my homies. Kel came by and grabbed me on the ass. I got so mad that I went to my class, and, the whole time, I was thinking about how I was going to get Kel. The bell rung and trade school was over.

I ran back to the dorm, and I grabbed the push broom, which had a metal bottom. I was acting like I was sweeping the floor until I saw him walk through the door. I walked up toward him, and I start unscrewing the broom. And that's when I went off.

"Pussy ass nigga! I told you to stop fucking with me." I yelled.

I hit him and the broom broke. When it broke, it broke into a point. I was just about to stick him in the neck.

"Harrison!" The officer screamed out and hit the stick out my hand. "10-10!" He called on the radio. 10-10 is the code meaning "Hurry! A fight just broke out." All the officers ran to the fight. When they heard this, they are ready for action, ready to beat you down, because they don't know if it's an inmate fighting with another inmate or an inmate and an officer fighting. They come running from all over the compound with blackjacks out.

The officers came in, and I was going off, cursing, yelling. "It ain't over nigga. I'ma get you again."

He was out of it.

I was taken to see the doctor, which we call the medical floor to get checked to see if I needed some treatment. If not, then the officers will take you to the lockdown dorm until you go to a disciplinary hearing, which we called "D.R. (Disciplinary Report) Court."

Yes, they had a system where they listened to see what caused us to fight or whatever happened. You go forward, then they will tell you if you get to go back to the dorm or whether they will give you "hole time," which is what we called it on lockdown. That's what I got, hole time, being that I was the new inmate on the block. He went back to the dorm, and I went to lockdown for fourteen days.

In the hole, they take everything from you, and leave you with a few underwear, T-shirts, and towel, and they bring you soap and toothpaste. The only other thing you were allowed in the hole with was a

Bible or Qur'an. I sat there in my cell for fourteen days, where I read the whole bible, praying, hoping to be out of this hellhole in three years.

"Inmate Harrison, you're going back to the dorm. Pack it up." An officer said.

"Where I'm going?"

"Ahh, Dorm 14. That's where you were. Right?"

"Yeah. Why am I going back there?"

"Man, this is out of my hands," he said. That is what the officer would say. "I'm just taking you across the yard," meaning back to the dorm.

I packed up my stuff, then we went to another part of the block or lockdown dorm to pick up the rest of my things. I walked around the corner getting ready to go back to the same dorm I left.

Kel was in there. He came to the front while I was sitting on the floor outside the bars. He came up to the bars and said, "Let me talk to you man. Man, I don't want no mess!"

I stated, "Naw dog."

He said, "I just want to talk to you about the situation."

"Cool."

The officer opened the door to let me in the dorm and told me to go to Bed 33. That was the same bed I left from.

"Oh well, I'm just trying to make parole," was the only thing I kept telling myself.

Kel came over, "Look, man. I apologize. I should not have tried you. We cool?" He asked.

"Yeah, I'm cool," I told him.

But every night I would wait until he went to sleep before I would go to sleep. I never took my eyes off him. I didn't trust anyone in that place. One night I woke up, and I kept hearing moaning, and the bed making noise, so I played it off like I was going to the bathroom. When I turned around to pee, I saw about four guys, who kept going in and out of a hut they made around a bunk bed with some blankets. A few minutes later, a white boy looking like a girl came in the bathroom to shit.

Another guy came in behind him and told him to, "Hurry up. My turn. My turn." At first, I didn't understand why he was rushing him or saying, "My turn." There were other toilets open.

I thought to myself, "What the hell is he talking about?" Then it hit me: They were taking turns having sex with him! "Oh hell, Naw! I gotta get out of prison. This shit is crazy." Now I was worried. "Oh, Lord Jesus! Get me the hell out of here please! Please Lord Jesus!"

The next morning, a guy I knew from Avondale High School named J.J. came into the dorm.

"Man, what's up, J.J.?"

"Man, Willie. How you get in here?"

"I killed my friend by mistake, and I plead guilty to life."

"Life?! Were you high? Crazy? Or just stupid?"

"Man, why you say that?"

"Man, you never getting out of here."

"They told me I'll be out in three years."

"Who told you that shit?"

"The public defender."

"The P.D.! Man, Willie, you really messed up your life. You couldn't afford a lawyer?"

"No, man."

"Damn, homie, I guess this will be the last time we will be together cause you in for life. Look. Let me put my food in your locker. I don't have a lock yet."

"Ok."

Now I was laying on my bed wondering if he was telling the truth or was the public defender telling the truth. "He doesn't know." I told myself. "They wouldn't lie to me. They know the law. They uphold the law, not lie about it." These are the words I was rehearsing over and over in my head because I'm getting out in three years.

A few weeks had passed, and this big guy came into the dorm by the name of Jerome. Alto had a system that, if you were from Atlanta, then the officers will put you in Dorm 14, or "the dog pound," as we used to call it. Across from us was Dorm 13, "the country dorm," guys from South Georgia, places like Albany, Bainbridge, Macon, Augusta, etc. Dorm 10 was the mixed dorm, with mainly guys who worked in the kitchen. Jerome was from the country.

If you get into it with the white officer, or if you were just rebellious, they would put you where you didn't want to be." Alto was an all-white officer prison, except for a few "Uncle Tom" niggas called the fords, fathers and son. But other than them, the rest were white racist officers, every last one of them. They hated niggas, but they loved to be around, hoping that a riot would break out, so they could come and beat the shit out of some niggas. That's how they get you, waiting for you to fight.

Anyway, Jerome came over to my bed. I was told to never talk to the country niggas, so I was kind of reluctant, but, I figured, "What the hell?" Then I started seeing guys getting together, putting their shoes on. In prison, that's a sign that trouble is brewing or that there is tension in the dorm. In my mind, I'm like, "What the hell's going on?" I told Jerome I would talk to him later. "I'm not trying to get into trouble I'm trying to make parole." I told myself.

Within minutes, they were jumping on him, sticking him with shanks, and he was knocking them out. Then, while he was fighting them, he looked up at me as if he was telling or asking me to help, so I just got up under the blankets, and the officers ran in.

"Everyone on their fucking bed now!" The officers yelled.

Jerome was lying on the floor almost dead. The officers went out with Jerome. However, the dorm had cameras, so they came back in about thirty minutes later and started telling guys to pack it up. E.J. was one of them. I was glad because it was like everyone was afraid of him. I didn't know why. He was human just like me. Weeks had passed, and one of the guys in my dorm got into a fight with the country boys, so guys started walking around the dorm with a list asking everyone, "Who's going to fight tomorrow?"

I said "yes," because I didn't want them to think that I wasn't down. But in my mind, I wasn't down. I was trying to make parole in three years.

"Yeah, man. I'm down. Let's do it."

Nighttime came, and I was just lying there thinking and praying, "Lord Jesus, please don't let me have to go out and fight."

"Five a.m. Get up ladies," is what the officers would say. They would come around to everyone's bed, hitting them with their blackjacks. "Get dressed."

Everyone would get up and go brush their teeth. Well, not everyone. Some guys believed that, if you brush before you eat, it takes the taste out of the food. We all would just go downstairs and eat pork, grits, eggs, and juice. The juice they gave us was called "peety wee." They gave it to us to keep us from getting "riled" up or to keep everyone from having sexual desires.

After chow was over and everyone was putting their trays in the window to the dish room to be washed, we headed back to the dorm, so we could get ready for trade school. But I saw guys putting big jackets on and stuffing their pockets. I pretended like I was getting ready, too

"Harrison to the front!" The officer called me. "You're going to the medical floor for a checkup."

"Okay." I ran to my bed, made it up, and made sure my locker was straight. Another officer was waiting to take me to medical.

"Man, thank you, Jesus." I thought to myself.

45 minutes later, we heard the codes for 10-10 being called on the officer's radios. "10-10! 10-10!" "10-10" is the code for a fight. I was hearing it going down, and I was glad that I wasn't there when it went down. But I was also just sitting there wondering why we were always fighting each other. "Why? We were all from the south! Man, we were hating and killing each other because of where we were from, but we all lived in the south.

I just minded my business. I was trying to make these three years. I just used to wonder, if I was free, what would my life

be like. When I went back to the dorm. It was half empty. A lot of guys got shipped to different prisons, so the guys that were in the lockdown dorms came into our dorm. A lot of them were just waiting on bed space.

Christmas time came. That's the time when everyone can get Christmas packages from their families. My grandma loved me so much that she would send me whatever I would ask her to send. She sent me some towels, pajamas, and food. Christmas packages made everyone feel loved.

The officers called me to the "intake room," as we called it. That's where everyone came through when they first arrived at the prison. It was also where the packages arrived. Someone called me to intake. My grandma sent me everything I had asked for.

One night, I was asleep, and I heard something behind me, but I didn't think anything of it. The next day my locker was open again, and everything from my package was stolen. That was the last straw. I couldn't take it anymore. They had tried me to the point that I was about to really hurt someone. I started yelling, "Everyone get the fuck up! Who the hell went into my locker? I'm sick of this shit!"

I started walking around the dorm looking for my stuff. I found some in the trashcan, some on top of lockers, some on the floor. This guy called "Brain" started looking at me. I stated, "What the fuck are you looking at, nigga?" He was a punk anyway.

"Nothing," He said.

"I thought so."

Ray, my homeboy from the Meadows stood up

for me, but I didn't need him. I was tired of this mess.
I went and got my bible and threw it out the window. I
then stated out loud one more time, "If any one of y'all
niggas fuck with my shit again, I'm just going to pick
anybody. I'm tired of this shit."

From that point on, I was fighting and taking
people's property. I just gave up and forgot about
those three years. Six years had passed, and I was up
for parole in November 1996. My counselor called me
to his office.

"Sit down, Mr. Harrison. I have a letter for you
from the parole board."

"Ok, good." The counselors were never
authorized to open letters. We had to open it in front
of them so they could see our reaction. If we showed
any sign of wanting to injure someone or just snap,
they would call the officer to take you to lock down or
isolation until they felt you were capable to go back to

population. I opened the letter, and it stated, "The Board's decision is to deny parole at this time. The Board determined that your parole release would not be compatible with the welfare of society due to the severe nature of the offense(s) for which you were convicted." It indicated that I would be eligible for reconsideration in 2004.

I just sat there, looked up and said, "Jesus, this what I prayed for, to be here longer." I just politely got up and went back to the dorm, laid down up under the covers, and cried. "Ok, maybe in 2004, I'll make it." But what if everybody was telling the truth about me having a life sentence? That I'll never get out? Was I too blind to see what I was sentenced to? "Oh well." Until then, I started being part of the system: smoking cigarettes, drinking Windex, smoking weed, etc. anything just to calm the rage inside.

I was hurting, but only Jesus and I knew it.

Every night, I would lie there, calling out to Jesus and asking him "Why?" Jesus was all I knew about religion. I was raised as a Seventh Day Adventist.

I was placed in school so I could take my G.E.D. The next day I got up and went to school. There was this new guy who had this jewelry on. I asked him if I could see it. After he let me see it, I never gave it back. I went back to Dorm 14. He was from the "country dorm," Dorm 13. He told his homeboys, so it was "gonna be on" the next day.

There was this place called the "catwalk," in the prison. It was one way in, and one way out. You would have to really fight. I was stabbed in the stomach by one of the guys when we were fighting. At the same time, fighting also was fun. We used to laugh about it afterwards when we all went on lockdown. It was crazy. We were all young and foolish.

When I came out of lockdown, they sent me to

the "VRC" dorm. That's what we called the dorm for good people. People were placed in VRC if they were assigned to outside detail. They didn't have much time to serve, only 3-4 years, then they would be back on the street. A lot of them would be back in prison again shortly thereafter. It was still part of Alto, so I was shocked when they put me in VRC. I thought I would never end up in VRC with a life sentence.

I went to Dorm 16. By then, I had a name for myself. People would say, "Lil Willie is crazy as hell." I just didn't care anymore because I thought "I'm never getting out, so why should I care?"

I was going on the yard and working out. I gained weight by working out. I was 5' 5", 185 pounds. I was just "getting it in," still trying to maintain. I was hoping every minute, every second, that they would call me up to get my short card, but it never came. When it didn't come, then I'd think, "Oh well, back to the system."

My homeboys were in the dorm with me. One of them, Omar, was my friend from my young teenage years. We start "kicking it." Then my homie from the Meadows, Rodney, came in the dorm. He had words with this dude. I saw them arguing and I just swung and knocked the other guy out. I felt that, if you were my homie or if we were tight, then I was going to go to bat for you. The officer called, "10-10," and there I was, back on lockdown for 21days. e

On lockdown, I was sitting there, trying to read other books. I couldn't really read or write that well, so I just stuck to the Bible, which I thought I knew how to read.

"Mr. Harrison, pack it up. You're going back to the dorm."

"Where I'm going?"

"Dorm 15."

"Okay."

That was still part of VRC, so I would still get in the dorm with my homies. When I arrived, all my homies were greeting me, getting my bags, and taking them to my room. We were just cool like that.

A few weeks had passed, and I was going to school trying to pass the pre-G.E.D. It was the hardest thing I've ever been challenged with. It was like I just couldn't seem to pass that pre-G.E.D. I was in school for about three years just trying to pass that pre-G.E.D. After that, I gave up on school and requested the trade school brick mason class, and I started doing that for a while.

Back in Dorm 15, I used to walk by a room, and I would see guys getting together side-by-side, bending over, and putting their faces on the floor. I didn't know that they were Muslims or that they were praying. I thought that was crazy. I just went into the

TV room and started watching TV.

I got real cool with this guy from Augusta named "Black." We were spades partners, so we would just gamble all the time until one day, when we got into an argument about the game. We were in the TV room, and he started getting loud, and "Bam!" I just hit him in the mouth. He was taller than me, and he was getting the best of me. "10-10" was called, and we were back to lock down. 14 days in the hole.

I went back to reading the Bible again, praying, and hoping that Jesus Christ would hear me this time so I could go home.

"Mr. Harrison, pack it up."

"Where am I going?"

"Dorm 10."

The kitchen dormitory. That was cool with me. There were a lot of guys that used to be in Dorm 14. When I was in that dorm, we used to gamble all night.

I would break into people's locker boxes because I hardly ever made store call, and, on the weekends, my stomach would touch my back. The Georgia Department of Corrections was just feeding us two meals on the weekends. I would steal guys' stuff until one day this new guy saw me break into someone else's locker. I guess he thought that, if anyone ever breaks into his locker, he was going to know that I would be one of the suspects. And it just so happened, I would be.

Months had passed, and I just got tired of doing wrong. I came back from the kitchen one morning. I used to be the baker, so I had to go in late at night to mix the dough for the biscuits in the morning. When I came into the dorm, everyone was up looking crazy. The lights were out, but there were lights on in the aisle, so I went over to Mike's bed.

"What's up? Why is everyone up?"

"Man, someone has stolen the new guy's stuff?"

"Who?"

"Man, you know who."

"Kenny H!" We said it at the same time.

"Oh, I should have known."

"Well, I didn't see it."

"I'll see y'all in the morning. I'm tired."

I went and laid down, and the next thing I knew, I was getting beat in the head and face with a lock.

"Hey, nigga! What's up!?" The new guy said, as he beat me while I was asleep.

"Get that nigga! He just jumped on Lil Willie," was all I heard.

I was messed up bad. I had to go to the medical floor to get stiches on my head, and my teeth were chipped. He messed me up bad. After they took me to the medical floor, they took me to the hole.

This time, I sat there in my cell thinking about God and my life and family, just wondering how my life would have been if I never went to prison. All kinds of thoughts were going through my head. At one time, I wanted to be a lawyer because I wanted to help people.

We were poor and I never really saw Christmas. Well, I never believed in it, because we never got anything. It's a good feeling, though, when you do receive a gift or present from someone you know.

After pondering, I just started crying and asking Jesus, "Why me? Why me Jesus? Please, Lord, forgive me!" Then, I went to sleep.

"Mr. Harrison."

"Yes, sir."

"Pack it up. You're going back to the dorm."

"Which one?"

"Dorm 6. Didn't you put in to be in a dorm for

THEY GAVE HIM LIFE

classes?"

"Yeah."

"So, pack it up, and let's go."

"Cool."

I got to the dorm, and I was next to this brother named Shahid. He was a part of the Five-Percent Nation. It was like a religion, a sect that broke off from the Nation of Islam. We got close. We talked a lot, and we became close friends until one day when we had a disagreement.

I got angry about him preaching his religion, so I threw this book against the bed and went into the TV room. He thought about it and ran in after me.

"What was that about?", he asked when he came in the TV room

"Man, you got that." I told him. Shahid was known for stabbing this guy in the neck. He was from New York and came down here to Georgia and got caught up.

Everyone was telling him, "Lil Willie going to end up hurting you, man!"

He asked, "Hurting who?"

"Man, please!" I told him. "You got that. I don't want to do nothing."

Later that night, we started back talking and laughing.

One night, we were talking, and I kind of saw him scratching or playing with himself while we were talking. In my mind, I was wondering, "What the hell he doing up under his cover while we talking? Is he killing [jacking off] my voice?" I grabbed his cover and pulled it off him, and we laughed like crazy. No gay stuff. We were true, hard brothers, very well-known in Alto

On Fridays, he went to Jumu'ah. Jumu'ah is the Friday Congregational Islamic prayer service. In prison, Muslims would go and listen to an outside chaplain come in and speak. They would pray this certain way which I thought was strange.

They came back to the dorm one Friday and Shahid wasn't the same. He started studying this green and gold book called the Qur'an. His whole life was changing right in front of me, and then he started trying to convert me.

"Naw, man. If it isn't Jesus, then I don't want no part of it," I told him.

Shahid had a way of making you look at yourself and question why you did what you did.

Months had passed, and this guy named Eric came in the dorm. We got cool, and we started working out together, and eating soups and pies together. He was from Macon, Georgia. He was bigger than me, but he always felt like he could just say anything out of his mouth to me. One day, he called me, "Fuck nigga."

I told him, "Watch your mouth."

"Man, fuck you, nigga."

We started arguing, and guys came over and got between us.

The officer came and stated, "Harrison, go up to the front of the dorm."

As I was about to walk toward the front, he stated, "Fuck nigga."

I ran back toward him and just started swinging on him. The officer was between us, but I didn't care. I was hitting the officer and trying to swing around to hit Eric, and the officer fell. When I looked down, Eric hit me, and I fell on one knee. I was out for a second. When I came to, I start swinging again. He got a good lick in on me. "10-10" was called. I was back to the hole for 14 days.

This time, I was able to come back up to Dorm

6. One day we all went out to yard call. A few of the crew that hung together, Shahid, and I were out there playing basketball. We were about to go in until someone called "O" had to really use the restroom. He had to really shit. They had a restroom on the yard, but people were pissing on the toilet, so he was holding it. We were trying to call for the officer, but he was taking his time letting everyone out so once we all came out. O ran to the dorm. The guard called for him to wait, but O wasn't hearing that. Everyone started telling the officer that O had to use the restroom.

"Inmate! Come back!" The officer called out. He didn't want to listen to us.

O didn't want to listen to the officer, so the officer tried to go toward him, but we cut him off. We stuck together. When we got to the dorm, the officer was in the back of the dorm, and O was yelling,

"Officer, come open the damn bars. I got to shit, man."

The officer started walking toward the front and opened the bars. O ran in, but by the time he pulled his pants down, he shits all over the wall, his pants, and the floor. From then on, we called him "Doodoo." As a matter of fact, we started calling each other "Doodoo." I was coming from church one Sunday, and I had drunk some milk for breakfast, and it hit me. I started running back to the dorm, but I didn't make it. I shitted all over myself. I was so embarrassed.

One weekend, my mother and sister drove from Atlanta to visit me. I knew they were coming, but it just so happened, we had this real racist officer working the dorm that morning. I left my ID on my bed so I had it ready to grab when they called me, because you couldn't go to visitation without having your ID.

"Harrison," the officer called me to the front. "You have a visitor. When they call me for visitation, I got my pants from up under my mattress, because that's how we use to press our clothes. When I went to get my ID card, it was missing. I knew I put it on my bed. Someone told me that they saw officer Alison around my bed, so I went and asked him if he took it. He said he didn't get it, but I didn't believe him. I went into a rage. I started cursing the officer out, and they called, "10-95," meaning "officer down."

They came running, and I was going off. "You racist mother fucker! You know you got my ID!" I was so mad. I hadn't seen my family in years, and he pulled this stunt. I went to lockdown for six months.

"Harrison, pack it up."

"Where am I going?"

"Dorm 16."

"Oh ok."

I got in the dorm, and O, Shahid and all the crew were there. I was back to gambling, smoking weed, drinking alcohol, and stealing. I just got wild. I just didn't care until one day the counselor called me to the office, and he asked me to sit down.

"Okay. What's up?"

"I have some bad news to tell you. Your grandma Bessie has passed."

I got up and knocked the counselor's stuff off his desk and onto the floor, and I started cursing him.

"Calm down, Mr. Harrison."

I sat down and just stared at the ceiling.

"You okay?"

"Yeah, man. She was all I had to support me."

I went back to the dorm and told my homies. They just sat there quiet. When guys get bad news, they go and get on their beds, get up under the blankets, and cry. No one says nothing. They just wait until they come out and start back talking.

A few months had passed, and the counselor called me to the office again. This time, it was to give me a letter from the parole board. Once again, it stated "The Board's decision is to deny parole at this time." I went back to the dorm, got on my bed, and just stared.

Prior to this day, Shahid used to always come to me and talk about Islam, but I was not listening. It got to the point where, one time, we were in the hallway of Dorm 16, and I told him "I don't want to hear about no religious shit," and he just walked away.

On this occasion, I laid down on the bed, and he came up to my bed and whispered in my ear, "Just pray to God."

And that's what I did, and God heard me!

Months had passed, and I was walking down

the hallway one morning, and I saw him reading this green and gold book. I walked over and asked him, "What are you reading?"

He told me, "The Quran."

"What's that?"

He started explaining to me about Prophet Muhammad and Islam, and it was very interesting to hear. I started to think about what he was saying about Islam.

I was so excited with what he was saying that I went to my bed and just stared at the ceiling.

I was wondering: What is this new religion called Islam. Why not give it a try? I gave Jesus a try all my life and look where I ended up. Jesus didn't save me from catching a life sentence.

The next day, a brother brought me a book, *Muslim-Christian Dialogue*. I asked, "What's this?"

"Just read it," He said. "It will help you to make

a decision. It's your life, brother. You are in control of your own destiny."

When he said that, I went to work like I was in college and studying for an exam that would give me millions once I passed!

I was so engulfed by what I was reading that I forgot that I was in prison. A brother named Hakeem gave me my first Quran. I read it every day. This book gave me so much hope and life. I started to compare verses with other verses, because, when I read *Muslim-Christian Dialogue*, it compared Bible verses and showed some comparisons that didn't add up. I decided to do the same thing with the Quran, and it was adding up. I was trying to find faults and discrepancies within the Quran, but I couldn't.

I started learning about the Prophet Muhammad. Who was this man? What was his mission? I started questioning my life, my purpose as a man, and as a human being.

Islam had influenced me to the point that I went to Shahid and Malik and said, "I want to be a Muslim. What do I need to do?"

"You just need to confess that there is no God but one God, and you believe that in your heart, and you will be Muslim in the eyes of God!"

In August of 1997, my life was transformed, and I saw life differently. I wanted to attack Christianity. I was angry because I believed that I was only following what my Mom taught me to believe. She thought that was best for us, and I didn't blame her. She was only raising us to know that there is something far greater than we are. I couldn't thank my mom enough for that, but at the end of the day, it was between me and my God, not my Mom. However, I was still stuck between a rock and a hard place. I wasn't fully transformed into a Muslim.

One time, Deante called me into the room with him and Trey. "Man, what's up?" I asked.

"You want some weed?"

"Hell, yeah. Wait till I get out the shower."

"Okay, cool."

A few minutes later, Deante called me in the room, and he was putting on his clothes, and the weed was on the top bed on the side. By the time I picked it up, this white officer came by the window and saw it. I tried to hide it, but it was too late. He came up, and he asked, "What's that?"

"What's what?"

"That!"

"I don't know what you're talking about!" I knew right then that it was time to go pack up my stuff because, once he takes that joint back to his desk and opens it, I was a goner.

I walked down the hall and told Mike, Shahid,

and Omar, "I'm going back to the hole."

They asked me, "For what?"

"Man, I'm going back to the hole."

This time the officer called me into this room and said, "Lil Willie, where did you get this from?"

I told him, "I got it off the floor in the dorm."

What they wanted me to do is tell them what officer was bringing it in, but I just kept telling them that I found it. Sgt. Jack told them to put me in lockdown until I told them where the weed was coming in from.

I said, "Cool."

I stayed in lockdown for about six months. I didn't care, though. I had my food brought to me. I had books from the library brought to me. They came around to my cell and asked if I wanted a shower. I was in chain gang heaven. I had a life sentence, so I didn't care that I was locked down. I started to reflect on different things.

I had started to reflect on what Shahid had told me about Islam, and it really started to sink in my head. After my six months was over, I went right back to Dorm 16 and almost back into the same room. I went to talk to Shahid, and, before I knew it, I was saying I bear witness that there was no God, but Allah and that Prophet Muhammad is the last Messenger of God. Months passed, and I started learning Islam.

One morning, the officer came to my bed.

"Lil Willie."

"Yea, what's up?"

"You're transferring." "

"What?"

"Yeah, man."

"Where am I going?"

"I don't know, man. They don't tell me nothing. When you get to the bus, they'll let you know."

I went to tell Shahid that I was getting transferred.

"Where to?"

"I don't know yet, but I'll write you once I'm there."

I then went to tell Mike. "Yo, Mike. I'm out, man."

"Ok, just hit us back, and let us know how life is."

"Man, I'm still locked up. It ain't like I'm going home.

On my way out the door, I just had to turn around and get one last look at my homies. "Love you guys. And thanks, Shahid. Man, you saved my life. Man, I will never forget you."

"Brother take care of yourself. We gave each other a hug.

As I walked down the hall, I yelled, "I'll holla

man. I'm out."

I gladly walked to the bus. After spending eight years in Alto, I thought I was never going to get away from that place. I had started getting mad at the officers. I hated officers so bad. They used to think that they could talk to any black person any kind of way, and I was getting to that point that I might have done something to one of them and gotten away with it. I started plotting on how I can beat an officer down or bust his head. I started thinking crazy thoughts a lot of time.

People on the outside, mainly the parole board, don't know what the prisoners go through, being harassed by officers all the time. A lot of time, those officers used to come in the prison with the mentality that "These are not people. They are only inmates. They are nothing, so treat them as such." An officer told me this. When I first went to Alto, there were mostly white officers, except for two black officers who we used to think of as "house niggas." One of them named Cole is now locked up himself for killing his wife. But that's another story.

On the bus, Officer Jack said, "What's up, Lil Willie?" Officer Jack said. We used to call him that, because he was a jackass, and he just got used to it.

"Man, where am I going?"

"Well, it looks like you're going to Phillip State prison."

"Okay. Where's that?"

"Phillips is in Buford."

"Man, that's close to Atlanta." I was thinking that I might be going home soon, since I'm close to Atlanta. A lot of times guys used to think like that psychologically. We used to play tricks in our head, or, should I say, keeping hope alive. Anyone with a life sentence would think that way. All we had is hope, being that your life is in the hands of the unknown, that is, the parole board: people we never saw and who never saw us, except for an identification photo in our parole file.

On the bus, I was shackled with someone else. Everyone knew "Lil Willie," so I had no problems being next to anyone. A lot of those guys at Alto were probably glad that Lil Willie was gone. I just didn't take BS because I figured, "I don't have anything to lose. I'm in for life." That was my mentality.

The bus left before daybreak so, by the time we arrived at Phillips, it was around 9:00 am. We pulled up, and officers were standing around. As we got off the bus, they would tell us to go into the ID room. We had our pictures taken, then they told us to get undressed and get into the showers and put this type of shampoo around your private part in case you had crabs, lice, or something similar.

Afterwards, I got dressed. They gave me new clothes and boots, and we sat for about three hours in a cell before an officer came around to tell us what dorms we were going to.

"Harrison."

"Sir."

"You going to G-Building, room 12, top bed."

He then called another prisoner. "Joe."

"Yeah?" Another prisoner responded.

"Yeah?! Who do you think you talking to, inmate? You say, 'Sir.'"

"I'm a grown man. I say what I want."

"Okay. We got a smart ass." The officer got on the radio and called for the CERT team, and they came: four big dudes deep.

"Yeah! What's the problem?" one of the CERT team asked?

"We have a smart ass."

"Who?"

"Joe."

"What's your problem, inmate?"

"Nothing."

"Well, you address the officers here as 'sir.' Do you understand me?"

"No."

"What?!"

"I said 'no.'"

They threw him up in the air and on his head. They beat him down bad and told us to get out of the ID room. This was common in prison when beatings occurred, as guards didn't want witnesses present. Outside, we could still hear him hollering as they beat him

Months had passed, and I saw him around the prison one time. He looked like a zombie. They had drugged him up so bad to make it look like he was a problem. It was so depressing to be in such an environment where officers could do what they wanted to you, and they had no conscience about it. They would just sit around and laugh about what they just done to you. The world doesn't know about this. The world needs to know the deal on these people, the other side of the criminally minded: officers behind the fence, behind the badge.

After being there for a few months, I was next door to this old man called Mr. Moore. He was always in the law library. One day, around 4:00 pm, we were about to get counted so the officers came in and yelled, "Count time. By your door. Everybody out."

Once count was over, I went to worship In Islam, there is a difference between prayer and worship. Worship is offered at a set time of the day that a Muslim should give Allah. That's what the angel Gabriel told our Beloved Prophet Muhammad. (Peace

Be Upon Him.)

Mr. Moore said, "Hey, man. What's your name?"

I said, "Aqil." Once you become Muslim, brothers will give you an attribute, a Muslim name. Mine was Aqil, meaning one who struggles to hold back from wrong things.

"Man, what's your real name? I don't know about that Muslim stuff."

"Willie."

"When count time over, come and talk to me."

"Okay."

He was over there smoking, and we started talking. We became real good friends.

One day, he asked me what I was in for. I told him, and he said, "You in school. You ain't trying to fight that life sentence?"

"No."

"Why not?"

"I did the crime, so I'll just wait until they let me go."

"Let you go?! Are you that stupid? Do you actually believe that the white man is going to let you out of this shithole?"

"Well, I hope so." I said.

Mr. Moore just shook his head. Then he said, "Man, we're going to the law library tomorrow, and I want to show you something about that life sentence."

"Ok." That night I lay in my hard bed thinking about my life and wondering was there still hope. After talking to Mr. Moore, he really had me thinking now.

Being away from that young prison, Alto, I was now around older men. Alto was about a lot of young guys who only thought about gambling, sex games, and doing drugs. That place was designed to keep young black men down, and mentally corrupted.

The next day, chow call was called round 6:00 am. Around 8:00 am, first block was called, meaning that it was time to go to school, trade school, or yard call, but the main thing was you had to get out of the building so that the dorm orderly could clean up before inspection started. Mr. Moore and I went to the law library.

He started showing me things about life sentences. I was so stunned that I just sat there and stared into space. I was badly misrepresented by my public defender and I became very angry after I explained to him what I did and how my public defender did me. He said, "It's called ineffective assistance of counsel." He started showing me what that meant, and that was it. He said, "You need to get to work so you can cross examine her."

I asked him, "How will I be able to do that?"

"You'll have to file a habeas corpus."

"What's that?"

He started explaining it to the point that I got discouraged. I never had the will power to believe that I could do anything or be something in life. Prison had made me become so negative. Mr. Moore said he would help me get started. He told me to start getting all these types of paperwork from DeKalb County Courthouse. When that paperwork started coming in, I couldn't believe what I was seeing. My public defender really railroaded me. She just wanted to get the case over with by getting me to plead guilty.

Mr. Moore said, "Youngblood, "This won't be easy. You will have to really show the court that she really messed you over. I mean dead to the right."

I worked day and night on trying to learn this law thing. It was hard, but what I was training my life for was determination, drive, and ambition. I never thought that I had such will power. We all have it, but we will never see our full potential until we are placed into a vital situation that we truly don't want to be in. That's when we will realize that it's time to fight for your life.

Being in prison with a life sentence, you don't own your life anymore. What if I was ever free? Every day I was in fear of being free. A police officer could kill me, and I thought about this every day. I had a fear of leaving my house, wondering if I would be killed one day by a white police officer who would definitely go scot-free for the murder of Willie C. Harrison Junior. This was a hard pill to swallow. People don't understand what I fear on a daily basis now. I'm speaking on behalf of all convicted felons. If an officer were to randomly just stop me, and he's in one of those killing moods, and he looks me up and see that I'm a convicted felon—that's if they were to ever stop me—they could shoot me and get off scot-free. They could say that I had a gun, or I just got violent. With all this killing going on with officers killing black people, I fear for my life. Every day I woke up I felt these thoughts in prison. We are nothing in these officer's eyes. Dead meat. An embarrassment to the black race. We failed our race while they're trying to uphold their own is what they think. That's why they don't mind killing us. Black officers started acting like white officers.

I started fighting hard on my case. I started to feel burnt out, so I decided to relieve myself by going out and playing basketball. I got in another fight and had to go back to the damn hole. Most of my fights came from playing basketball. People who know me will truly laugh because they know that I'm telling the truth. While I was sitting in the hole, reading my Quran, and learning to memorize chapters, a few weeks had passed.

"Mr. Harrison, pack it up."

"Where am I going?"

"What dorm did you come from?"

"G-Building."

"Well, that's where you're going back to."

"Okay, smartass."

"What did you say, inmate?"

"Huh?"

"Never mind."

I went back to the same dorm. I went to talk to Mr. Moore, and we started back working on my case again, but this time I started going around the dorm asking other people about the law and trying to get their outlook on the law and what was the best route to take. This guy named Richard B. was a doctor, so I started talking to him about my case and he started helping me. We started going to the law library. He was doing more of the work. I couldn't believe it. We worked day and night on my case. We started rehearsing in the TV room. Waseem and Richard were really preparing me for a habeas corpus.

The Muslims in the dorm used to call for prayer, so I would stop and go pray, then come back and rehearse. It was a hard process, but I had to try and fight my case. I was still in school. I was even in auto body shop, but now my mind was focused on getting my case overturned. I was afraid, but no matter what, I wasn't losing anything. I could only gain. I was still fighting and going to the hole.

I was going to Jumu'ah Islamic service every Friday. One day, the older Muslim there told me to get up and speak. I went back to the dorm and started learning everything I could. I was nervous, but I was ready. At least I thought I was. When I got up in front and I spoke, God was really with me that day. I really felt good about myself, something I never felt before in life. From that point on, I realized what my reason for living my life was: change for the better. I started educating myself by reading the dictionary.

Reality still hit me from time to time that I was still locked up, and I wanted to be free.

I had my habeas hearing. My sister Reebe was there, and she said that she was very impressed with what she saw. She could see as well that the judge was impressed. After going into the courtroom twice, the judge still denied my case. I was disappointed, but my buddy, Mr. Moore told me, "Youngblood, you did your best, but don't forget that prison is still the white man's world."

"Yeah, you're right."

I was transferred to Hays State Prison where I ended up in a lifers' group program, learning and trying to stay clean from fighting. Once again, I ended up in the hole for fighting. But when I got out the hole, I went back to the lifers' program.

My mom and sister started coming to see me in 2004. I was coming up for parole again, and I was telling my older sister. She decided to hire an attorney. He came to see me. He asked me questions, and I showed him a letter that I had been sending the parole board. He asked if he could keep it. After he was finished, he took my letter and just put his title on it and sent it to the parole board.

A few weeks later, the parole board wrote me back using the same form letter that they sent me in 1997, saying the same thing. I just went back in the dorm after leaving the counselor's office. I cried so bad. I just wanted to die. This time the letter said I was not eligible for parole until 2012.

My Muslim brother came in my cell. "Akhi," he said. ("Akhi" means "my brother" in Arabic). Shariff,

"I'll pray for you. I have a life sentence, too.

I was transferred about two more times until I went to Central State Prison in 2007. I had been in prison 18 years. In the back of my mind, I often wondered, "Will I ever get out of this place?"

I spent my time praying, going on the yard, running for hours, going to the library, studying, reading books about business, and talking to brothers on a daily basis about how it would feel to be free. I would lay on my bed at night writing in my journal, thinking about family, about how I wanted to be married, what type of business I wanted, and hoping that I would be able to make it to Mecca for Hajj (Islamic pilgrimage) before I leave this world.

I knew I had to get my G.E.D. This guy, "White Mike," and I became close friends. We started challenging each other. I told him I refused to let a white boy prove that he's smarter than me, and he said he refused to let a black person outdo him. We were in the same dorm. We slept across from each other. It would be late at night, and I would lie down but I would see his light on. I used to peep over there, and I'd see him studying. I would then start studying myself. We were up for nights studying, determined to pass the G.E.D.

I took it about twenty times and failed, but, in my mind, I often thought, "What is the purpose of getting a G.E.D.? I'm never getting out." But I also said, "What would it hurt if I did get it?" I studied harder than I ever studied for a test.

When the big day came, Mike came up to me and asked, "You ready?"

"Yeah! Are you?"

But deep down inside, I was nervous. Fear kicked in again, but I prayed, and I went in doubtful, but I still gave it my all.

A few days later, my name was no longer on the school list. I asked the officer, "Why?"

He said he didn't know why my name was not on the school list anymore.

I asked him if I could go see why I'm not on the callout list for school. Also, to be honest, I didn't want to be in the dorm for inspection. I went to talk to the teacher, Ms. C."

"Good morning, ma'am."

"Hi, Mr. Harrison. Congratulations! You passed the G.E.D."

I couldn't believe it. My heart just fell to the floor. Mike had passed as well. I went to the yard and screamed my head off. I never believed in myself. I had doubted myself for so long to the point that I believed that I could never do anything right. I now felt that the fact that I passed that G.E.D. proved my outlook wrong. I knew I could do anything I put my mind to. Being in prison clouds your mind sometimes.

I passed, and I couldn't believe it.

CHAPTER 11
CULTURAL SHOCK

April 28, 2010.

"Mr. Harrison, pack it up," the officer told me.

"For what? I haven't done anything." I got nervous because I didn't feel like packing my stuff and going to the hole. I told him, "I'm not doing nothing. You come and pack it up."

He was smiling, but I didn't see anything funny, so he said, "Man, you're going home."

I said, "Man, go ahead on with that. I have a life sentence. I have three more years before I come up for parole."

He said, "Well, it must have come early."

I was getting mad now and so was he. He told everyone to come in from the yard, and he called the warden down and another officer. "10-10" is what they called it when there was serious trouble.

I was standing there ready to fight who ever

came in and tried to take me to the hole.

"Come on in here, Mr. Harrison," the warden said. "Will you calm the hell down? Just come with me to intake and let me show you something.

"Okay." I came out and let them put the handcuffs on me, and we walked to intake and to the front gate. There was my mom.

I went back to the dorm and packed my property.

As I was walking out, the dorm officer, Talib, came out with me, grabbed my hand, gave me a hug, and whispered in my ear, "Keep in touch, brother. You're gonna make it!"

I pulled away and looked at him. "Thanks, man."

"I was never against you." he said.

I ran back to intake. As I was changing clothes, there was an officer who always harassed me, and had me jumped on, but I never gave him a reason to. I think he just hated Muslims, or he was just on the wild side. In any event, he was trying to make me so mad, but I just looked at him. I was escorted out the gate, and my mom and my son Donterio, (who I had before I went to prison) were sitting in the car waiting for me.

When I got to the car, I opened the door, and my mom said, "Get into the car, son. It's over."

I just cried all the way to Atlanta. I just couldn't believe I was out of prison. I looked back and cried. It didn't seem real. "How? Is this a dream?" I just started questioning myself wondering if this is a trap or a dream.

We went to go get me a phone. I had about $35.00 and this card they give you. 21 years and all they gave me was a bus pass and $35.00. What a combination. "Oh well, I'm home now. It doesn't matter," I thought.

Now the real story is that I was supposed to be going to my aunt's house, but I was told that I had 24 hours to report to the parole board, so I was spending time with my son and my mom. My aunt started calling my mom's house. My little sister answered the phone, and my aunt start cursing and yelling, "Where the hell Junior at? He was supposed to be over my house. Why the hell he over there?" She was going off so bad that I felt like going back to prison because I felt like, if she came over, then she was going to kill me. I was thinking, "Did I do something wrong?"

My mom and my dad's side of the family kind of fell apart. Once my dad and mom divorced, the whole family just went they're on way. My mom's and my dad's sides of the family stopped speaking for over 30 years until I came home. When my aunt came to pick me up from my mom's house, it was a reignited fuse. It just escalated. It was so heated that my dad came into my mom's house and told me to get my stuff and "Let's go."

My mom was trying to talk to my dad, but he acted like he didn't want to hear from her. He started yelling.

My wife, Michelle, at the time, was there. Michelle and I met through my mom about a year before I was released. We got married five months after I came home. She surprised me and my mom because she brought me clothes, shoes, etc. No one knew that she was going to do that for me. What a blessing, but I'll get to that later. She was standing there while I was collecting my things. She told me that my dad was talking to my mom crazy. She thought they were about to fight, so she was ready to throw down with my dad if my dad would have made any false moves, but nothing happened.

My son Donterio and I got into my aunt's car, and she started cursing me out. Right at that moment I wished I never came home. I was so upset. My son called my mom and was just holding the phone letting my mom and Michelle listen to her just cursing me out. She was stating, "Do your ass want to go back to prison? You are in my custody. I'm in charge of you. Now do you want me to send your ass back to prison?"

"No ma'am."

"I'm doing all this for you, and you supposed to be over at my house. I got everyone over there, and you over your mom house."

And the bad thing about it was that she didn't ask my mom if she could come. I called back over there, and my wife Michelle told me that my mom was so upset, but more so, hurt. She said they just went out and ate.

I was not prepared for this to happen. I thought

I knew my aunt before I went to prison. We were close, but people change. I saw I was in for a culture shock and the beginning of a rude awakening.

After living there for three days, I was getting horrible treatment. Every day, when my aunt came home, she would call me to her room and start crying, telling me, "I can't do this!"

In my mind, I was trying to figure out, "Do what?" I asked.

"Do what?" She started telling me that she couldn't take it that I was there, and that it was hard for her to deal with me living there.

In my mind I was thinking, "Then why did you tell the parole board that I could live here?"

The next day, she came home asking me do I need some money and what I would like for dinner tonight.

Then the next day, she called me downstairs to

tell me, "Sit down." Then she started telling me what bills I needed to start paying.

I just got out, I'm on a leg monitor that I have to pay $95.00 a week for, so I was begging my family for money. I was walking around door to door, asking people if they could hire me to clean up their yard, going to different jobs and filling out applications. I had to be out of the house during the weekday before 5:00 a.m. and back in by 5:00 p.m. I had to walk around with this form that the parole board gave me to verify that I'm out looking for a job. It was very devastating. I didn't even have any money for bus fare.

Then my parole officer told me that I had to take a class MRT (Moral Reconation Therapy). I told her that I took that class in prison, but she told me that it didn't count.

Plus, I would have to pay for the class.

Every day it was getting harder and harder.

On my way back home from looking for a job, I asked someone if they could drop me off on Northside Drive, and I would walk the rest of the way home. By the time I got into the house, my aunt would call me to her room, and there she went again. She started crying and telling me that she can't do this, and I need to find a place to stay.

I was so confused and upset that I called my mom and sister crying to them. They were telling me to just hold on. By this time, too, my wife, Michelle, was coming over bringing me food and seeing how I was doing. She would go back over my mom's house and tell her that I was doing okay which I wasn't. I was going through straight hell.

That Wednesday, the parole officer told me to come in early. We had to talk about why I had not found a job. When I got there, I had to sit in the lobby and wait until my name was called.

"Mr. Harrison." She came out and called me after I had been there for about five hours. That five hours would have been better spent by letting me go out and look for work rather than wasted sitting in a lobby waiting room. I was very exhausted.

I told her, "I'm trying to find a job. It's just that I have to wait until they call me back."

She told me, "You will have to take a class Thursday."

"I'll be here.

"Here is your form. I Hope you find work today."

This was Wednesday. On Friday morning, my parole officer called me with an attitude and told me to bring my behind into the office ASAP. I was thinking, "What have I done now? I'm out looking for a job. What now?" I got there, signed in, and waited another 3 to 5 hours waiting to be called in. When she called me in, we went into the chief's office. In my mind, I was thinking, "What was this for?" When I got into the office, the chief aggressively told me to have a seat.

I was like, "Okay."

He just started yelling, "What the hell is your problem?"

"What do you mean?"

"Why the hell didn't you come to class?"

Oh my, I just remembered. "Sir, hold on, hold on. I have been going through hell. I don't know who talked to my aunt but she's under the impression that she had to put up her house for me to come home. I was crying because, in my mind, I was thinking they were about to send me back to prison. My mind was racing. I was thinking of how I could get out that door before they tried to send me back to prison because I promised myself, I wasn't going back. But my parole officer was at the door, so I dropped that thought, because I was not trying to catch another charge. One was enough.

"Oh! Mr. Harrison, we didn't know," said the chief.

"Yes, sir. I'm catching hell at home. I just got out on Monday, and its Friday, and I have been going through hell, and I'm tired."

"Look, if you have somewhere else to go, just take the box and call us to let us know where you're going to be, and we will go from there."

Michelle told my mom that I'm not going to make it there with my aunt so she told my mom that I could come live with her.

After I got out of the parole office, I walked across the street to look for a job, and my aunt called and told me that she couldn't take it, so I needed to leave within the next two months.

I said, "Okay."

I called my parole officer. "I just left the office, and she's calling me, crying and telling me that I had to leave."

The parole officer told me to leave and just call her once I got to where I was going.

I called Michelle and asked her if she could come and pick me up from aunt's house. I was out of there in about a minute flat. Oh, how I was so glad to be out of there.

But no matter where you go in life, there are always going to be difficult situations, and what I was looking for was for everything to be easy but living with my then-future wife wasn't easy. She just tried something, not knowing what to expect from a guy she barely even knew.

This is how we got to know each other in the

first place. In 2009, I called my mom, and Michelle was at her house helping my mom pack because she was moving. My mom told me to talk to "my sister." Sister?! She's a sister that my mom never told us about, and that I never knew existed. I was shocked, but happy, at the same time.

I started talking with whom I thought was my sister, and I could hear my mom laughing in the background.

I was wondering why my mom was laughing so much, so I asked, "What's so funny?"

My mom replied, "She is not your sister. I was just joking." She got me.

Michelle and I stayed in touch. I was calling her regularly, and she tried to come and see me, but the prison wouldn't allow her. I was upset. The officer knew me, but they said that she wasn't on their copy of the visiting list, even though she was

We started talking to each other and getting more acquainted. I told her that I was going to marry her.

She flat out said, "no," because I had to "get my life together."

I said, "ok."

We stopped talking because my cellphone got confiscated by the guards during a shakedown.

In 2010, five months after I got out, we were married. We had to move around from place to place because, due to my background, a lot of apartment complexes didn't want convicted felons, let alone convicted murderers, to live there. We went through a lot of obstacles. I was getting discouraged because I was still wearing the monitor on my ankle.

My wife started applying for jobs for me through temp services. I was working at one temp agency for a while, and they wanted to hire me... until they realized that I had a criminal background. I just kept going to different temp services.

One of my homies told me about one job, so I went there, and they hired me. My background didn't matter to them. I was there for about a year and a half.

Michelle and I found a place to stay, then she got laid off, and I started working three jobs. I was exhausted, but I had to do what I had to do, and I was determined to make it. I started getting burnt out, especially being on the bus line working three jobs.

Then I lost all three jobs. We were moving from place to place. I was getting tired of all the moving. We moved to Jonesboro in a nice house. I had started a small lawn care service.

One day I was getting ready for work. I was putting my lawnmower and other stuff in my trunk. I ran back into the house to get some things, and

Michelle was getting into the shower.

"I'm leaving for work, Love."

"Okay." she said.

By the time I opened the door, a guy was trying to come in my house. The old gangster in me kicked in. I turned into a lion. He took off running, and I was on his tail yelling at him. "When I catch you, I'm going to kill you. You done messed up now. You came to the wrong house." He must have known the area because he ran behind this house and jumped over a fence. He got away and even though my wife called the police and they came and took an incident report, they never caught him.

We didn't want to live there anymore, so we moved into my sister's place. A lot of people were living there: My mom, my younger sister, and three of my nieces were living there. The house was big. It started getting terrible.

We went out on faith, and we moved to Buckhead, one of the richest places in Atlanta. We would go out to restaurants and just try to enjoy our marriage, but we would still have our moments with religion and our ways still trying to get to know each other.

That's life. I've realized that, no matter what, in a marriage, there is compromise. There will be ups and downs and disagreements but at the end of the day, you two still will have to eat, talk, and sleep together. You have to be honest with yourself, and I had to learn that, after being out of prison for years, I wasn't truly honest with myself or with her.

Michelle knew when I came home that I was Muslim. I was in the kitchen, and I was going back into the bedroom when I heard her telling someone on the phone, "If he doesn't get baptized, then he got to go."

I was still fresh out of prison, not knowing how to really do anything, so I thought for a second that, "Maybe if I get baptized, I could stay, and she would marry me. Okay. That's what I'll do. Get baptized." However, in my heart, I felt this feeling like, if I just hold on, it would be okay. But I suppressed that feeling, and I got baptized, and my life wasn't right ever since because I did something that I didn't feel comfortable doing.

I started drinking every day. I was just going through it a lot. I started going to different organizations, such as Atlanta work force development, and Urban League of Greater Atlanta.

This lady named Ms. Ruth heard about me. She filmed a documentary on my life called "I Paid my Dues" and put it on You Tube. I started going to the juvenile detention centers and telling the youth about my life story. My older sister gave me a car so I could get around. Then when I started getting laid off so much, Michelle paid for me to take a CNA class. I passed with the highest grade in my class and was given a gold pendant. I felt so good about achieving this. I started applying for CNA jobs and when I went to the interview it was going well until I was asked if I could pass a background and drug test. I said I would pass the drug test but not the background so the manager asked me to explain. I was really selling myself but that was when the hiring manager for this CNA position stated, "unfortunately the nursing home don't hire convicted felons."

The parole board doesn't care about all the other stuff. The only thing they care about is, "Do you have a freaking job? Are you working, or are you going back to prison?"

After being frustrated and let down from being let go from so many jobs, Michelle asked me if I would like to be an extra in movies and I thought, "Why not? I can't keep a job." My first movie was "The *Flight*" *starring* Denzel Washington, then in a sitcom, *BET* "*The Game.*" This is just a few of the movies or shows that I have been an extra in: "*The Watch*", "The *Originals Constantine*", "*The Vampire Diaries*", "*Ride Along* 2", *Tyler Perry's*, "*The Haves and Have Nots*", and two stage plays. Although I couldn't find a job, the movie and television industry didn't care about my criminal background.

I was working as an extra for months until I got a job through my close friend, Duck. He told me that he knew this guy at a company called Wegman. I went there and applied, and they hired me that same day. I was the warehouse manager, and things were going great. I finally had a stable job, with no worries, especially with the parole officer not on my back. I started getting familiar with the other guys, and I started driving the company truck out of town on a regular basis. I was feeling this job. A year had passed, but things went from bad to worse. I got close to the wrong people, and they started having a bad influence on me. I've learned that I give my heart to people too quick, and that's been my downfall a lot of time with people. I eventually left the job after having been there for almost two years.

I went back to being an extra. I got a role in the movie *The Watsons Go to Birmingham*. I was just looking for jobs. I learned how to really use the computer, but my wife was doing all the research, and she was applying for lot of temp jobs for me. They were loving me, but when they wanted to hire me on permanently, they would call me into the office and tell me to sit down and have me thinking that I'm about to be placed on a good job. Then the employer would tell me that although I was one of their best workers, they would have to let me go because of my criminal background and that they wanted to hire me, but it was out of their hands.

I would just sit there, and I'd think about the letters I was getting from the parole board repeating to me why they didn't think that I was suitable for parole. This job thing was going the same way. I really started drinking.

Then my wife was laid off her job and things started really going downhill for us. I started getting mad with her for no reason. I would call my mom and complain and pour my heart out to her, and she would just say "It will be alright Junior."

In my mind, I didn't want to hear that.

My wife and I were moving around from place to place. I stopped drinking when I saw that things were going okay. But during the times that I felt like I was going downhill, I would go get a drink. I started hiding the drinks from my wife.

We moved into a house in Jonesboro, and someone gave me some money. I bought a lawnmower and started going around putting fliers on doors. I would put my lawnmower in the trunk of my Saturn and get to work. I earned enough money and got me a weed eater and other things to do the yards. I was feeling good about myself... until I stop paying the $30.00 monthly parole fee.

I don't know why I had to pay this fee. I guess it's supposed to be an appreciation fee, to show our appreciation to be free. One day I received a phone call from another parole officer telling me that I needed to come in, so I went in. He told me very abrasively to sit down. They always come off abrasive, until they find out you're a pretty good person, one that they don't have to worry about.

He came right out and said, "Why haven't you

been paying your fees? It looks here that you owe $360.00. Do you have it? Because I need this money ASAP, or we will have to place you in the county jail until you can come up with it.

I called Michelle and told her what was going on and she brought the money. Now I really had to find a job just to recuperate from having to pay those fees. Being on parole was stressful, but I just kept looking.

I never thought I'd be living in such nice places, but my wife got a permanent job, and I landed a job with a landscape company. They didn't care about any background, as long as you could cut grass. There were illegal Mexicans there, so it was cool.

My wife and I started having problems again, and, this time, I had to let her know I couldn't keep on pretending that I believed in Jesus like she did. She looked at me and said, "ok."

I felt like my life was going downhill unless I started being true to my heart. I was stressing myself out, and I didn't realize that until it start hitting home.

We started out real rough, but it got a whole lot better. At one time, I felt that it would be best if I left so I could get my life together. I was willing to just step out on faith and deal with the world. A lot of my friends were telling me that I never gave myself enough time to get adjusted to the world. I just jumped into a marriage, but that was what I wanted to do. I just wanted to make it right, and I thought that maybe the woman I ended up marrying would not only accept me as a person but also my belief.

All I wanted to do was just live life and be free, do things, and venture out, but being on parole wasn't going to allow me to do that. I will just continue to dream and pray that God will allow the parole board to take the leash off my neck so I can run free.

Five years after I got out, I applied for a pardon. I asked several prestigious people to write letters on my behalf. They included a doctor, a police officer, a pastor, and several more people. The pardon form asked me to explain my case and I did. A few months later, I was denied a pardon. It wasn't unusual. It just reminded me that I had to do another eight years to get off parole. I was disappointed, but I should have expected that from them. My name wasn't pulled out of the hat like they usually do. The pardon representative told me to apply after five more years.

The world needs to understand that, when people get out of prison, their intention is not to end up back in prison. We only want to redeem our life back, even though it will take time to do so. Being on parole makes you feel like you're in prison, with one foot in and one foot out. Curfews make you feel like a child.

The truth needs to be told because taxpayers pay for this message. If you want the truth, here I am not biting my tongue. A lot of times, people are always trying to be so careful, but if we never speak out, then how will you ever know how we feel as ex-cons? It's terrible. It's heartfelt and heartbreaking when I'm living this life.

Yes, I committed a serious crime, but what about doing the time? Does that matter? I also have to pay to be free. Isn't that double jeopardy?

But the key to not getting stressed, it is to understand that I'm blessed. Blessed to be out of prison but not free, and to be able to walk out of my door, to go into my refrigerator, and to not have to have a male roommate that's in your room.

After being locked down for twenty years, I just thank God for this opportunity to just say, "Thank you, God," and to continue to strive for success.

I was on Iyanla Vanzant's show in 2017. What an experience. I thought I fixed my life, but she really exposed a lot of things in my life, and I could never thank her enough for having me on the show and for just enlightening me about life. Now, instead of putting things behind me, I stand on it, I did it, I take full ownership for the things I've done. I'm sharing her message to the world of youth. Now I'm building a portfolio, so the next time I write the parole board for a pardon, they will reconsider.

I want to say to families that lost a loved one or have been victimized that I'm sorry for the loss of your loved one. I was a teenager with no parental guidance. I'm not trying to make excuses; I'm just sharing the facts of when I committed my crime. I wasn't in the right state of mind.

When I sat in prison, I just couldn't believe

what I'd done and why. But when I allowed my heart

to be opened, I saw the light in my life. I will never

know why because I realized that's not for me to know

or decide. I just have to continue to deal with life's

struggles and understanding my purpose in life. I will

continue to reach out to young people. I don't care

whether they are black or white. Everyone needs help,

especially our youth. The times when we feel like

everything is okay are the times when we need to

press harder in life. I'm truly hard on myself, but I

know that, that only makes me better and stronger. I

know that the struggle is real, and I will never take life

for granted again.

<u>Conclusion</u>

God is my source of life. God allowed me to see

life for what it's worth, as opposed to what it is. I'm

truly glad that I went to prison. It opened my eyes to a

lot of things about myself, such as the strength I didn't

realize I had inside of me and the ability to achieve things that I didn't think I could accomplish. I realized that God helped me to see people for who they are and to respect people regardless of diversity. We were created differently for a good reason, and, if we just take the time and turn around with open eyes, then people will realize that God is right there in your face every time you see a person. So how can you disrespect, or abuse the image of God? That person you judge has the ability to do as you do, breath, feel, see, etc. All that we have is truly a blessing. Prison helped me to pull out of my heart the true essence of God and be more appreciative of God's gifts to me. That's the love that I have for you. Thank you for reading this book. I could have never done this without the people of this world, so thank you, until the next one.

The End, My friend.

I love you.

In Loving memory of Willie C Harrison Jr

J.W. Jones Jr.

ABOUT THE AUTHOR

Willie C. Harrison Jr, a resident of Atlanta, Georgia, is happily married to Michelle Harrison. At age 17, Willie C. Harrison was charged with Murder & Armed Robbery and was sentenced to Life plus 20 years in prison. At age 38, after spending 21 consecutive years behind bars, he was released. It's been almost 10 years since his release from prison. Unfortunately, Willie faced many challenges after incarceration such as finding employment, finding housing, learning how to use a computer and cellphone and many other electronic devices, getting re-acquainted with his family and friends, adapting back into society, suffering from PTSD (Prisoners' Traumatic Stress Disorder), being shunned by family, friends and others and just the initial shock of being free. However, Willie made a conscious decision, post-incarceration, to be a crime-free, productive citizen and an asset to society. Willie has some great accomplishments that he's proud to mention such as the fact that he's now a mentor to at-risk youth & young adults, he often visits prisons and detention centers to speak to the inmates and tell his story and to encourage & inspire them, he has a full-time job as a delivery driver and is also the Vice-President at a new 501c3 charity organization in Atlanta, Ga, named '4 My Destiny Community Arts Center Inc' which is a performing arts center for at-risk youth & young adults, he's also a first time home buyer and has purchased his first new vehicle, Willie & his wife often volunteer at local nonprofit organizations, Willie also was featured on the season finale of "Iyanla Fix My Life" in November 2017, on the OWN network, where he was able to tell his life story, he also has been an extra as well as a featured extra on many movies and sitcoms that were filmed here in Atlanta, Ga, Willie frequently attends many events, seminars and workshops here in Atlanta that focus on Empowerment, Business & Entrepreneurship, the Criminal Justice system, Social & Civil issues, etc. In 2014, Willie & Michelle Harrison started a new Film Production company named "XCONS of ATLANTA" (What are they doing now). The purpose of this company is to film, follow and document the life stories of men and women who have been released from prison, after serving long periods of time, sharing their journey about what led to them being incarcerated, what issues did they face while being incarcerated, what challenges are they still facing after their release, what did they want to become in life, had they not been incarcerated, what have they become, their success stories, etc. XCONS of Atlanta also volunteers and gives back to the community, have support group meetings & empowerment sessions, assist X-cons with resumes, referrals and resources for housing, jobs, counseling, etc. Our mission is to help, assist and empower ex-cons in every way possible and to encourage them to lead positive and productive lives post-incarceration and to let the world know that people do make mistakes and bad choices that often land them in jail or prison, but they can make a change for the better and make the right choices and live a great, productive life and make the world a better place, one day at a time.

Contact Willie at:

willieharrison233@gmail.com

My Life Before

My Family

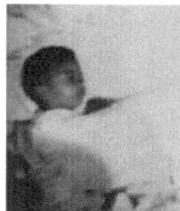

Me as a baby

My mom, Dr. Simmons,
my sister Maria
and me

The Harrison Crew

My Dad,
Willie C. Harrison Sr.

My baby brother,
Urian K Harrison

My son

My dad and my uncle
Aldo W. Harrison

My dad, sisters, my brother
and me.

Prison Life

17 years old and addicted
to crack cocaine

Phillips State Prison

Wheeler State Prison

Phillips State Prison
1999

Phillips State Prison
1998

Phillips State Prison 1999
My sister Maria, me and my
cousin Sarah

Georgia Department of Corrections

Certificate of Commendation

This certifies that

HARRISON , WILLIE 580195

successfully completed

MORAL RECONATION THERAPY (MRT)

August 31, 2009

at

CENTRAL STATE PRISON

S. BROWN

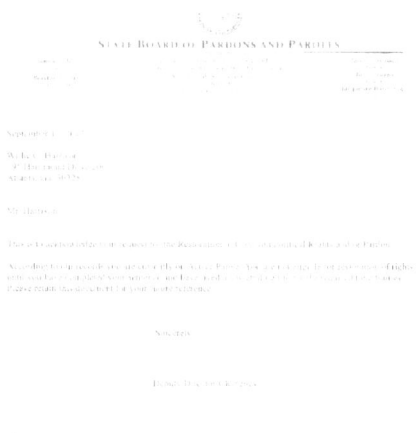

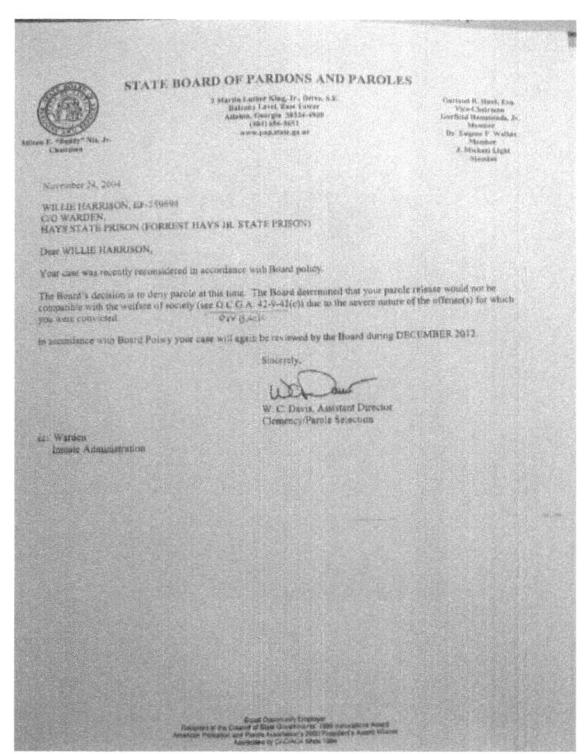

STATE BOARD OF PARDONS AND PAROLES

2 Martin Luther King, Jr., Drive, S.E.
Balcony Level, East Tower
Atlanta, Georgia 30334-4909
(404) 656-5651
www.pap.state.ga.us

Milton E. "Buddy" Nix, Jr.
Chairman

Garland R. Hunt, Esq.
Vice-Chairman
Gerffeld Hammonds, Jr.
Member
Dr. Eugene P. Walker
Member
J. Michael Light
Member

November 24, 2004

WILLIE HARRISON, ID-259698
C/O WARDEN,
HAYS STATE PRISON (FORREST HAYS JR. STATE PRISON)

Dear WILLIE HARRISON,

Your case was recently reconsidered in accordance with Board policy.

The Board's decision is to deny parole at this time. The Board determined that your parole release would not be compatible with the welfare of society (see O.C.G.A. 42-9-41(c)) due to the severe nature of the offense(s) for which you were convicted.   (SEE BACK)

In accordance with Board Policy your case will again be reviewed by the Board during DECEMBER 2012.

Sincerely,

W. C. Davis, Assistant Director
Clemency/Parole Selection

cc: Warden
Inmate Administration

Equal Opportunity Employer
Recipient of the Council of State Governments' 1999 Innovations Award
American Probation and Parole Association's 2000 President's Award Winner
Accredited by CA-CALEA Since 1984

Sonny Perdue
Governor

GEORGIA DEPARTMENT OF CORRECTIONS
Floyd Veterans Memorial Building
Room 756 - East Tower
Atlanta, Georgia 30334

Brian Owens
Commissioner

Date: 04/28/2010

RE:HARRISON, WILLIE
PAROLE CASE# 259694
GDC ID - 580195

Dear Warden:

The attached parole order or conditional release order authorizes the release of the above names inmate.

Be certain that the inmate understands the conditions of his or her release. Three copies of the order should be signed and witnessed. Return one copy to the Department of Corrections, one copy to the inmate and one copy for your files. Provide the inmate with the arrive notice and any other instructions. Release the inmate as directed by the order.

BRIAN OWENS, COMMISSIONER
DEPARTMENT OF CORRECTIONS

BY: _Barbara Neville_

Barbara Neville, Director
Inmate Administration

Note: If subject has been moved to another jail, return release documents and provide new jail county and date moved. If subject was released from your jail, return release documents and provide date and reason for release.

** SHOULD RECEIVE RELEASE GRATUITY

Entertainment did not care about my prison record

The movie "Flight"

The movie "The Have and The Have Not"

"Church Folk Got Issues Too"

Life on the outside

My stepdad Wibert Simmons and me

XCons of Atlanta

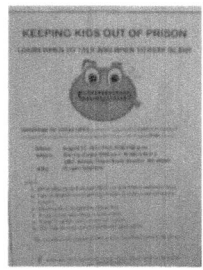

The

Boxer

www.ingramcontent.com/pod-product-compliance
Lightning Source LLC
Chambersburg PA
CBHW030326020726
47493CB00004B/1170